# SEVEN SPHERES

# SEVEN SPHERES

RUFUS OPUS

**Seven Spheres**

ISBN: 978-0-9905687-0-4

Published by Nephilim Press
A division of Nephilim Press LLC
www.nephilimpress.com

Copyright © 2015 Nephilim Press and Rufus Opus. All rights reserved.

No part of this publication may be reproduced, stored in a retrieval system, or transmitted, in any form or by any means, without the prior written permission of the publisher, nor be otherwise circulated in any form of binding or cover other than that in which it is published and without a similar condition being imposed on the subsequent purchaser.

# Contents

Preface: On the Genders of Kings . . . . . . . . . . . . . . . . . . . . . . . . . . . . 1

Introduction . . . . . . . . . . . . . . . . . . . . . . . . . . . . . . . . . . . . . . . . . . . . 3

Hermetic Cosmology . . . . . . . . . . . . . . . . . . . . . . . . . . . . . . . . . . . . 9
    The RO Take on the Hermetic Creation Myth . . . . . . . . . . . . . . . . . . 11
    The Chain of Manifestation . . . . . . . . . . . . . . . . . . . . . . . . . . . . . . . 14
    The Magician's Sphere of Influence . . . . . . . . . . . . . . . . . . . . . . . . . 16

Kings and Kingdoms . . . . . . . . . . . . . . . . . . . . . . . . . . . . . . . . . . . 19
    Kings: What Makes You One . . . . . . . . . . . . . . . . . . . . . . . . . . . . . . 19
    Kingdoms: Really, It's All about Kingdom Maintenance . . . . . . . . . 25

Jupiter . . . . . . . . . . . . . . . . . . . . . . . . . . . . . . . . . . . . . . . . . . . . . . . 29
    Jupiter Magic Overview:
    Why Jupiter Magic is GOOD . . . . . . . . . . . . . . . . . . . . . . . . . . . . . . 29
    Grace . . . . . . . . . . . . . . . . . . . . . . . . . . . . . . . . . . . . . . . . . . . . . . . . 31
    Applied Grace . . . . . . . . . . . . . . . . . . . . . . . . . . . . . . . . . . . . . . . . . 33
    Authority: Divinely Right Rulership . . . . . . . . . . . . . . . . . . . . . . . . 34
    Applied Right Rulership . . . . . . . . . . . . . . . . . . . . . . . . . . . . . . . . . 35
    Oh yeah, the Power . . . . . . . . . . . . . . . . . . . . . . . . . . . . . . . . . . . . . 35
    The Danger . . . . . . . . . . . . . . . . . . . . . . . . . . . . . . . . . . . . . . . . . . . 36

Mars . . . . . . . . . . . . . . . . . . . . . . . . . . . . . . . . . . . . . . . . . . . . . . . . . 37
    Rules and Governance: the Art of Kingship . . . . . . . . . . . . . . . . . . . 38
    The Art of War . . . . . . . . . . . . . . . . . . . . . . . . . . . . . . . . . . . . . . . . 39

The Sun . . . . . . . . . . . . . . . . . . . . . . . . . . . . . . . . . . . . . . . . . . . . . . 43
    Feeding the Kingdom . . . . . . . . . . . . . . . . . . . . . . . . . . . . . . . . . . . 44
    Into the Light, I Command You . . . . . . . . . . . . . . . . . . . . . . . . . . . 47
    The Assistant . . . . . . . . . . . . . . . . . . . . . . . . . . . . . . . . . . . . . . . . . . 50

Venus . . . . . . . . . . . . . . . . . . . . . . . . . . . . . . . . . . . . . . . . . . . . . . . . 53
    The Core of Venus Magic . . . . . . . . . . . . . . . . . . . . . . . . . . . . . . . . 54
    The Faces of Venus Magic . . . . . . . . . . . . . . . . . . . . . . . . . . . . . . . . 55

| | |
|---|---|
| Relationships | 55 |
| Pleasures | 57 |
| Production | 58 |
| Opulence | 59 |

## Mercury ........................................................... 61
The Flow ............................................................ 61
Classification, Correspondence, and Research ............... 62
Thought and Memory ............................................. 63
Mercury's Influence in your Kingdom ......................... 64

## The Moon ......................................................... 67
The Moon and the Shape of Things ............................ 67
Materialization .................................................... 68
The Moon's Forces in your Kingdom ........................... 69
    Vision ............................................................ 69
    Materialization ................................................. 70
    Follow the Light ............................................... 71

## The Sphere of Saturn ........................................ 73
Defining your Kingdom .......................................... 75
Working with Saturn ............................................. 76
Saturn's Forces in your Kingdom ............................... 78
    Binding .......................................................... 78
    Releasing ........................................................ 80
    Time .............................................................. 80
    Wisdom ......................................................... 81
    Cursing and Hexing .......................................... 82
Border Expansion ................................................. 83

## Ritual Planning ................................................ 85
The Schedule ...................................................... 85
Timing .............................................................. 87
A Walkthrough of the Rite ...................................... 91

## Ritual Preparation ........................................... 93
The Fixed Ritual Implements ................................... 93
The Mutable Ritual Implements ................................ 95
    Jupiter Conjuration Preparation ........................... 97
    Mars Conjuration Preparation ............................. 99

    Solar Conjuration Preparation.................................. 102
    Venus Conjuration Preparation................................. 104
    Mercury Conjuration Preparation ............................. 106
    Lunar Conjuration Preparation................................. 108
    Saturn Conjuration Preparation ............................... 110

THE SCRIPT .................................................................... 113
    The Orphic Hymn to Jupiter ..................................... 115
    The Orphic Hymn to Mars......................................... 115
    The Orphic Hymn to the Sun..................................... 116
    The Orphic Hymn to Venus....................................... 117
    The Orphic Hymn to Mercury.................................... 118
    The Orphic Hymn to the Moon.................................. 119
    The Orphic Hymn to Saturn ..................................... 119
    Closeout...................................................................... 120

TALISMANS .................................................................... 121
    The Nature of Talismans........................................... 121
        Types of Talismans.............................................. 122
    Talismanic Maintenance............................................ 122
        Initial Consecration: Activation of the Talisman.................. 123
        Initial Consecration Rite: Angelic Planetary Method ............. 123
        Scheduled Maintenance ...................................... 125
        Other Forms of Maintenance................................. 126
    Putting Talismans on Vacation ................................. 126
    Decommissioning Talismans..................................... 126
    Planetary Talismans .................................................. 127
        Jupiter Talisman.................................................. 128
        Mars Talisman.................................................... 130
        Solar Talisman.................................................... 132
        Venus Talisman.................................................. 134
        Mercury Talisman.............................................. 136
        Lunar Talisman .................................................. 138
        Saturn Talisman.................................................. 140

AFTERWORD: KINGDOM MAINTENANCE AND TAPPING THE POWERS OF THE
SPHERES TO LIVE AN AWESOME LIFE ............................... 143

# Preface:
## On the Genders of Kings

I think there is nothing more stupid than the idea that one gender is inherently fitter, better able, or more valuable than the others. Throughout this book, I use the term "King," and it is traditionally associated with those incarnated humans having a penis, and nothing else. I tried writing "Kings and Queens" every time, and that just got really awkward and clumsy. Also it doesn't address the many genders in between male and female that exist in the human sexual spectrum.

When the Gents for Jupiter were formed, it was decided early on that we would allow all Gents who determined they wished to honor Jove into the cult, regardless of gender. "Gent" became a matter of dignity, honor, and respect, and had nothing whatsoever to do with gender. I refer to all members, regardless of their physical equipment as "Mr. [Last Name]," because within the Gents, we are all equal and have no gender.

I feel the same about the term King. To me, a King is anyone who rules, regardless of their gender. The need for different words to differentiate between genders is silly, in my opinion.

I realize this is not true for everyone, and to those who are offended, I request you extend me a little royal Grace. When we meet in the flesh, you can tell me what you would prefer as your honorific, and out of respect for my fellow noble-born ruler, I shall call you whatever you like. Within these pages, I use King because I like how it sounds, and if you'd prefer it were another word, feel free to replace it as you go along.

Ultimately it matters to me nothing at all what lies between your legs; you, like me, were born a king.

# Introduction

*"Do not worry then, saying, 'What will we eat?' or 'What will we drink?' or 'What will we wear for clothing?' For the Gentiles eagerly seek all these things; for your heavenly Father knows that you need all these things. But seek first His kingdom and His righteousness, and all these things will be added to you."*

—LOGOS [Matthew 6:31–33]

I spent many years practicing Money Magic. I started with Archangels, who tried to tell me I needed to do some Work before they would help me. So I went to demons, and got an instant return on my efforts. And I also got the opportunities to do the Work the Archangels suggested. I tried Seals of Jupiter, and I tried Gator Hands; I did rites to gain favor of executive management, and rites of luck on my job searches.

And I was successful. I found a lot of different ways to make money. I could manifest up to $1500 in a couple of days, and opportunities for much more in a couple of weeks. The longer you're willing to let your plan build, the more you can make. It turned out that making money through magic is really easy once you figure out the secrets. Even now, I'm working on a project that will net me millions.

But the nature of money magic is such that it is not terribly effective until it is not terribly necessary. Stressed out magicians aren't thinking clearly, concisely, or effectively. They plan poorly, and as a result they do magic poorly. They have so many immediate needs that they end up spending all their time dealing with the little things instead of the bigger things that would solve all the smaller problems at the root.

I needed money all the time because I didn't understand how money itself worked. That's what the Archangels tried to tell me early on. I didn't have time to listen, because I really thought money was my biggest issue that needed to be solved, the panacea to all my concerns. And I had bills to pay. I was living like a Pauper, and I wanted to live like a King, and the biggest difference I could see between my Pauper self and Kings was that Kings had money, and I didn't.

What I needed to realize was that Kings aren't Kings because they have money. Kings have money *because they are Kings*. They don't get to collect taxes because they are rich and powerful, they are rich and powerful because they *rule their kingdoms*. Rulership is not simply telling people what to do. If you've ever worked for a boss that was like that, you know they were not very effective at leading their teams of people. No one wants to call the techniques of good management "Being a good ruler" because of the connotations that come with that, but the fact remains that if you rule your world like a good and wise King, you will find yourself receiving the benefits that come from Right Rulership.

The quote at the beginning of this introduction is attributed to Jesus "The LOGOS" Christ. He was basically talking to a bunch of people like me and you, all worried about bills and finances and things that have an expense. We need to pay taxes, we need to pay for clothes, housing, cars, food, and high speed internet. We need to pay for things.

So we go after money, because our desire for things is not a very good currency. We get focused on the things we need that we think will make us happy, and we go after the means to get those things. We go after money. Let's get a better job, more revenue streams, more income, more, more, more.

But the LOGOS pointed out something really important. The things we seek, they are part of what automatically comes with a kingdom. They are secondary manifestations, the results. Look at Kings. They have everything they need, and then some. LOGOS was saying, look, don't go after that stuff; that's what other people do with their lives, people who have not been chosen to *know who they are*, who have not had their divine nature and true paternity revealed to them. Instead of going after all that stuff, or the means to get that stuff, focus instead on the Kingdom. Learn that you are a King already. Learn what that means, learn the art of being the Royal You. Train

## Introduction

yourself, improve yourself, be Kingly, and you'll find that you have a Kingdom of a God all around you, and that you are its ruler.

But what are Kings?

Kings are people who were personally (or through the source of their noble lineage) positioned by fate and fortune and gifted with the quality required to lead their world naturally. They were linked to the gods either by favor or by blood, and they received a Kingdom as a result of their nature and the quality of their deeds. They were *noble*.

It wasn't until I had turned my focus and attention on the establishment of my own kingdom that I began to realize what it meant to be noble. It came to me when I started doing intense work with Jupiter that released a large wave of the Greater Benefic's forces into my life all at once. I received a great deal of good fortune, both spiritually and financially. I had joined the Gents of Jupiter, a semi-formal Mystery Cult dedicated to "sitting around in suits drinking whiskey and setting the world to rights . . . literally," and was pursuing that motto full steam. I did weekly rites to Jupiter on Thursdays, seeking communion with its intelligences and deities, initiation into its sphere, and the integration of the forces it represented.

In typical Jupiterean fashion, I was flooded with inspiration, opportunities, and opulent, extravagant experiences of great joy. What I received from the rite personally was a vision of the role of the Magician in his Sphere of influence.

I saw the Magician anointed as a King by the forces of Jupiter, and that the receipt of this anointing ennobled the magician. I saw that their "Kingdom" consisted of all the things, situations, objects, events, and people that they interacted with daily. I saw how the forces of each subsequent planet in the chain of manifestation operated in different aspects of the Kingdom, and how initiations into the planetary spheres changed the magician, making him a more effective King as he grew in power and understanding of the forces of creation in each of the planets and the things they represent in the material realm.

In the following sections, we'll be going through what that means in more detail. We'll start with the very basics of the Hermetic system I practice and teach. You'll be reminded of who you are and where you come from. You'll understand why you are, regardless of your current situations, a noble person of royal birth. Then we'll discuss the chain of manifestation, the secrets of how everything we experience in this material realm, from the color of our hair to our relationships, from our career paths to the cars we drive, come into being from nothing, and how they return to the nothing they came from. Then we'll go into the meat of the work of becoming a Magician King, and how you can activate the powers, wisdom, knowledge, and authority necessary to rule your Kingdom.

As you go through this process, you are going to experience a wide range of changes. We all want changes for the better, and in a year when you see where you end up as a result of doing this Work, you will be so happy . . .

But, as with every change, the process is not always going to be pleasant, or easy. Challenges arise, and you must face them. Consider yourself on a quest to become the King, and understand that you will face challenges along the way. These challenges change us, improving our skills. There is only on-the-job training in the Kingship game, unfortunately, but that's okay. There's nothing we can break that we can't also fix. We learn the right way of doing things by doing them wrong, in a myriad of brilliant, different ways.

This is why, when it came time to pick a name, Aleister Crowley chose for himself the motto, "Perdurabo," Latin for "I will endure unto the end." You are taking the steps to reclaim your essential divine nature, to become a Hero of legend. It isn't a walk in the park, or even a trip to the grocery store at 9:00 a.m. when all the zombie humans and their offspring are fingering all the produce and getting in your way. It's getting fired, and surviving months of unemployment miraculously, as you learn that money is easy and not what you really need at all. It's "losing" a toxic person you've struggled to build a life around because you felt trapped by obligations, and finding that you're now free to be with someone you can cherish, honor, respect, and live with in beauty and harmony in true partnership. It's finding responsibilities that drag you down are secretly sources of great joy and fulfillment.

In other words, it's not going to be what you think. It's not going to be easy. It's not going to be fun. You have the potential to lose everything you think you hold dear, and it might cost you your life as you know it.

Oh, but, brothers and sisters, that is exactly what you need. The things we think of as "our lives" are why we want to become Kings in the first place! If we were happy, we wouldn't want things to be better.

And chances are it won't be nearly as bad as my warnings imply. I want to warn you, just in case.

# Introduction

Regardless of the pains on the journey, I swear this to you: when you have reached the end of the journey and have learned the skills of Kingship, you will be so happy and thrilled that you look back in fondness on the process you went through to get there, even the parts that hurt.

So without further ado, on to the basics of the system.

# Hermetic Cosmology

Like many modern magicians, I came to the traditional grimoires by way of a twisting and arduous path. I started in Celtic Neo-Paganism and moved on to Golden Dawn style Kabalistic magic. Along the way, I read a lot of Crowley's writings, and while I think I benefited a great deal from his wit and insight, I thought I understood a great deal about magic and magicians in general that wasn't exactly true. It turned out that being able to understand when he was making jokes isn't nearly the same thing as being in on the joke. It took a while to understand that subtle difference.

While I thought I had a good understanding of what it meant to be a magician and to accomplish the Great Work, the truth is that I had missed the most fundamental truths about my place in the universe. In order to understand what it means to even be a magician, I needed to start with the basics.

I had help figuring this out. I would like to say the help came from my Holy Guardian Angel, and maybe it did, but if so it came through a rather un-angelic lens. I was participating in a lot of online occult forums, discussing my experiences and learning more and more about magic. I was pretty well-versed in the Kircher Tree depicted in Donald Michael Kraig's *Modern Magick*, and felt pretty good about my KBL chops.

Then I met a guy in Europe who challenged everything I believed. He had performed an extensive, long, slow meditation and contemplation of the Sefer Yetzirah. As he worked with this earliest source text of the Tree of Life and all of KBL as we know it today, he built his own Tree of Life based on his meditations of the verses.

He discovered in the process that there are some fundamental flaws in the Kircher Tree of Life most people are familiar with from the all-pervasive Golden Dawn influence on modern Western occultism. There are basic assumptions made in the model itself that don't hold up when you look at the details. The Naples arrangement of the Kircher Tree is simply disharmonic. The best argument for keeping it is that it makes everything simple and work out numerically, if you just ignore some basic elements of the Sefer Yetirah.

I argued fiercely with him for many months, and he systematically demonstrated the weakness of my understanding. We would fight long and hard, cursing and swearing and insulting one another's parentage, while still delving deeper into the subject we both loved. We developed a mutual admiration though, because in the process of arguing, we grew sharper, went deeper, had to do more research and construct real pieces of rhetoric on the scale of Plato himself.

As I learned the Golden Dawn's Kircher Tree was flawed, I started looking for the source of the flaws themselves. I found that between the Sefer Yetzirah and the Golden Dawn were many confluences of cultures and beliefs. KBL had gone through a transformation and expansion in the Renaissance, just as the grimoire traditions had. Christian and Hebrew mystics met in the Renaissance and exchanged information (and misinformation), forming the foundation of the Christian grimoires and Moses de Leon's *Zohar*.

The best encapsulation of the neo-platonic creation story that I've found is in the second book of *The Divine Pymander* by Hermes Trismegistus. It's simple and to the point. Christians like myself can identify enough parallels with the Genesis account of creation to feel at ease in it, and pagans can find enough other gods that they feel at home too. It's a good little catch-all, and that makes sense when you study its history.

The *Corpus Hermeticum*, which contains the Divine Pymander creation myth, was recorded in the third century AD. This was the time that Christianity was becoming what it is today, Gnostic sects had infiltrated most of society, and the graduates of the Athenian Schools of philosophy were still respected. These varied belief systems were bumping elbows and rubbing off on one another throughout the Roman Empire.

My understanding of the Creation myth of the Hermetic tradition is summarized below. I go into my own interpretations, but it is important that you read it for yourself and form your own understanding. While it may be fitting for me to tell you what I think, it is never fit for one King to tell another what to think.

## The RO Take on the Hermetic Creation Myth

In the beginning was the essential God-the-Progenitor, dwelling in perfect darkness. In that perfect darkness, God still and always resides.

By its nature, God radiates infinite, pure light, and within this pure Light all that we experience begins. Yet behind the light, within it and beyond its ability to illuminate resides the True Father, the Monad-progenitor from which all things begin. I refer to this being as God, because it's easier, and I call him "him" because it's convenient for me, but his nature is beyond gender, and beyond the ability of words to express. He exists *before thought*, before even the *idea* of ideas can exist, and within that state of being there are *no words*, not yet anyway. This is like when you've got the feeling of a thing that you want, but you haven't explored it enough to be able to express it yet, because you haven't put it into words. All the words about this state are approximate at best, though. The ones I choose are the best I can come up with. Yours will be more appropriate for you, but these work for me.

In *The Divine Pymander*, Hermes Trismegistus is given a vision of the creation of the material realm. Within the infinite light appeared a great darkness, smoking as if it were on fire. Out of the infinite Light leaped a "certain holy Word" and that Word joined itself to the dark mass of Matter that came into being. When this holy Word entered the darkness, the matter itself separated into four realms. Fire leaped up highest to be closest to the infinite light, followed by Air, which seemed to hang between the Fire and Earth-Water below.

Next, God created a Workman and seven governors, each with their own sphere, surrounding the realm of Matter. Then the Holy Word, Logos, leaped up and . . . something happened between the two. The Logos cohabited and consubstantiated (or possessed) the Workman. They became one entity, yet retained their dual nature. This entity then set the spheres in motion, and the Spirit of Nature within the World began creating a material copy of the spiritual heavens within the material world.

Meanwhile, God made Man in Its image. Man was the last entity created, after the material world and its self-awareness that became the Spiritus Mundi, after the Logos and Workman, after the Seven Governors of the planetary spheres, after all the entities that you run into in the eighth sphere and beyond. He was the youngest and most beloved brother of the family.

I don't know if you have brothers and sisters, or if they are older than you or not. Personally, I was the youngest, and while it's not entirely fair, I was totally the favorite. "Favorite" is not a word that I should use, honestly, because it implies a level of affection toward me that my parents don't really have, but there's a chance my older sister will read this one day, and I just wanted to make sure she knows that I really do believe I was the favorite. She always accused me of that, and she was totally right.

I have a couple kids. I love each and every one of them the most, individually. It's true, they are all my favorites, for different reasons. The eldest is the one who got the experimental parenting. The middle child got more refined parenting, but by the time the youngest arrived, well . . . There's a saying that goes something like, the first child you wrap in blankets and put down pillows before putting them in a baby swing at the park, the middle child you make sure has their helmet before they get on their bike, and the third child you yell at to turn off the chainsaws she's juggling, for crying out loud, I'm watching TV.

It's not really that the youngest is loved more; it's that the parents are over all the new-kid crap and have concentrated their efforts where they are most needed. The eldest sees the youngest "getting away with murder" in comparison to them, and hate it. Likewise, by the time the youngest arrives, the parents are usually in better financial conditions and can afford more stuff that the eldest didn't get, so the youngest looks spoiled. If you went to Sunday school as a kid, you may remember the story of Joseph and the coat of many colors. It's like that. His brothers sold him into slavery to some Egyptians, and I am quite sure my older sister would have too, because she never really forgave me for being born.

Fortunately for proto-human created in God's image, it wasn't anything like that. He got treated better, sure, but that was because he was made in God's image. No one else was. They took one look at us, and fell in love, because we reminded them so much of our mutual Dad.

First Man went off exploring first thing. He descended through the Seven Planetary Spheres and received a portion of the powers of each Sphere along with training in how to use those forces to create. The seven Governors of the celestial spheres loved him, and he loved them. He thought they kicked ass, and he was fascinated with the process of creation. After all, he was an extension and duplicate of the Creator God the First Father. He descended through each of the planetary spheres until he arrived at the edge of the material world, receiving instruction and empowerment from each of his elder siblings along the way, getting trained in the art of creation.

When Man came to the material realm, he wanted to see what lay hidden beneath the sphere of Fire, separated from the celestial realms and removed from the spiritual realms in a way that was unlike any of the other heavens. Parting the upper veil, Man peered into the world below, seeing through the clear elemental sphere of Air into the sphere of Water. There, reflected in its surface, he beheld his own image.

Remember, he was made in the image of the First Father, whom he loved deeply. Seeing the form of his Source reflected in his own image, he was immediately smitten with it, not because he loved himself, but because the First Father is so lovely in form and function.

The Spirit of Nature, meanwhile, was also observing this intrusion into her sphere. She saw Man, and saw in his image the First Father as well. She saw Man fall in love with his reflection, and understood. She made of the elements a form of the reflection in the waters, a statue as it were, and Man, seeing this, immediately entered into the material reflection and became one with it, even as the LOGOS had consubstantiated into the form of the Workman.

So it is that Man has both an eternal nature and a temporal nature, the immortal Spirit and the mortal Flesh. We are, in a way, a symbiotic entity. Many traditions separate the flesh and spirit and create an animosity between the two. In Hermetics, we see that the flesh is not the enemy at all, but a material harmonic of ourselves. It is an animal, like every other animal in the material world, but we, the eternal spirits, ride around inside it. I try to take care of my body, as it serves me well. And after all, they didn't ask for me to come along and cohabitate.

Within each of us, we retain that immortal spark of the Divine. This entity is the same entity that hung out with God, the Logos, the Workman, the Seven Governors, all the hierarchies of elemental and terrestrial spirits, and who first fell in Love with the form created by the Spirit of Nature. This spark within is what gives us "authority" over the elements and the seven governors. They love us and work with us because we are the image of God. We're co-workers though, not masters of legions of spiritual slaves.

In the Hermetic creation myth, we see that the embodiment of the spirits of humanity was not a fall, nor was it beyond our control. Hermeticists see the material realm as a place of beauty, a physical image of our spiritual home world. It was not created as a prison, or as an accident, or as a punishment. It was created in loving care, crafted as a material tribute of the heavens it reflects. It was created as a labor of love, and populated with the natural and material spirits the same way the heavenly realms were populated with the celestial deities and intelligences.

In the Christian creation myth, we see God creating the world and the form of Man, and then breathing life into Man. Man had no choice, had no prior existence. Man in the Bible is presented entirely as a creation, like a pot created by a potter.

But in the Hermetic creation myth, we see that Man was created Above, complete and whole in the image of the original Creator God. Before enforming itself in the flesh, it received a portion of each of the planetary spheres, and the power to use these forces in creation. Understand the difference: we are not unwilling creations; we are here on purpose. We are not powerless servants of Fate; we are the creators and shapers of destiny. It is through our choices that fate is made manifest. We are willing, intentional incarnations, free to create and enjoy and experience our worlds as we see fit.

Or . . . not.

We can also just sit around and experience what other people create. It is easier to sit and enjoy the work of others, but we don't have as much freedom to make it what we want. We are able to respond and appreciate, and that's cool too, but if you really want to make what you want in your life, it takes personal Work.

You have to do it yourself. No one does it for you.

## The Chain of Manifestation

Let's take a moment to review how the universe looks, from a human perspective. Remember, humans are divine spirits that were made in the image of god, who received the power of creation and manifestation from each of the planetary governors as we descended into the material realm. When we look at the rest of the universe at large, we are looking "up" at it from the material realm. And remember also that the material realm is a mingled result of the four elemental kingdoms. Because when you remember all that, you'll remember who you are and why you're here. It just takes practice.

Ptolemy's geocentric model of the universe laid out the basic cosmology of the system we use in Hermetic Magic. It's like our modern map of the Solar System and the orbits of our star's planets, but it's a spiritual model, drawn from the experiential point of view of human beings living on

Earth. It is drawn as a series of concentric circles, but each circle represents a cross-section of a sphere.

Think of it as similar to one of the images of the Earth we studied in school. They would show a half-Earth with the layers of the crust, mantle, and core all shown one within the other. Ptolemy's geocentric model of existence is similar, showing each of the spheres as concentric circles.

The circles represent spheres and layers of materialization. At the far end is the Sphere of the Prime Mover, the divine darkness in which God dwells. Then there are the spheres of the Fixed Stars, followed by the kingdoms of the seven planetary governors that you'll remember Man passed through on his way to the material realm.

In the center are the Elemental Kingdoms, the material realm in which we dwell.

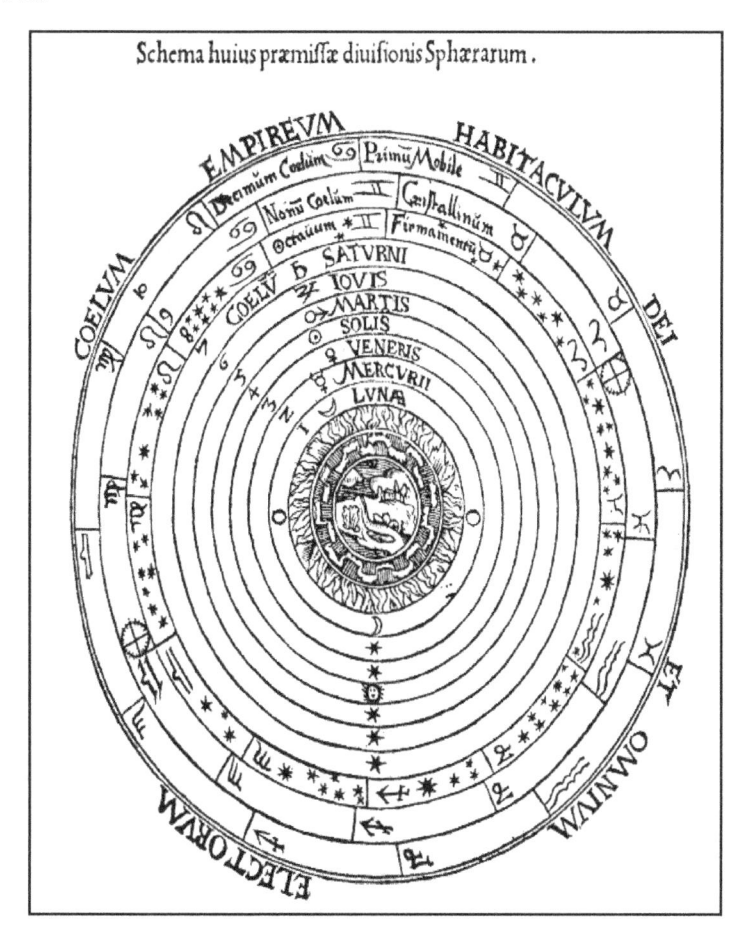

Anything that we can sense from within the flesh exists in the material realm. Anything we can experience in our daily lives that involves our physical bodies is taking place in the material realm. These central spheres in the map of the cosmology encompass everything that has matter, every person we know, and every situation we find ourselves in, as long as we are in the breathing body.

Everything that we experience consciously in the material realm begins as an Idea in the mind of God, and then descends through the spheres on its way to the material realm where it can be experienced by the entities of this realm.

As an Idea descends from the Mind of God, it passes through each of the seven Planetary Spheres and receives a portion of their essence. Everything that exists is made up of a mingling of various concentrations of the forces of each of the planetary spheres. When we say a thing is particularly martial, we mean that the forces of Mars are concentrated more specifically in that thing. However, that thing still contains in some small proportion qualities of every other sphere.

The combined essences of the planets are then projected into the Elemental World, where they take on the form that expresses the Idea and its celestial nature. The order of the descent is Saturn, Jupiter, Mars, the Sun, Venus, Mercury, and the Moon. This is the Chain of Manifestation. The phrase pops up in Renaissance astrological treatises and is the basic process of manifestation expressed in the Hermetic philosophy.

## The Magician's Sphere of Influence

Now I'd like to introduce a concept (and I don't claim to have created it) called "the Sphere of the Magician." Every one of us lives in a bubble of perception. Lots of us have read various modern and classical interpretations of existence that say all that all we experience is limited by that which can be sensed. Our nerves experience a thing and send electrical signals to our brain. Our brain processes these signals and converts them to "experienced reality." It's not an instant thing at all. The universe we observe and interact with is how things were a fraction of a second ago when the waves and particles were hitting our sense organs . . . yet we still think what we're experiencing is happening right now.

This bubble of perception is our sphere within the material realm. The Emerald Tablet of Hermes, an excellent model of magical operation on its own, bears the famous inscription "that which is above is like that which is below." Metaphysically speaking, we have a spiritual sphere of sensation as well as the physical sphere of sensation. They aren't really separated, but it's easier to think of them as parts than to try to understand the whole all at once. A seed in an orange doesn't look like an orange, and neither does the peel by itself, but they're still one thing.

This sphere of influence encapsulates everything we experience. We are at the center of it, processing everything that happens to us, enjoying the things we like, suffering through the things we don't like. We sit in a central command position within the center of our experienced lives monitoring what happens to us and deciding what we're going to do about things we're feeling and experiencing.

And that's the beauty of this situation. Our magical sphere is not only a passive thing. Sure, it receives input and we process that input, but based on that, we get to decide what we're going to do. We receive, but we also transmit. From the center of our experienced sphere, we can broadcast our pirate signal and hack into the matrix.

Ahem.

I mean, from the center of our experiences, we have the ability to decide what we are going to do, and then to execute those decisions in a way that changes the world we experience. This is how we create our world, through our choices and our subsequent activities. No matter what situation we are in, we can decide to do something that changes what we experience.

We don't have complete control over everything we experience. No amount of empowerment, initiation, training, or experience will ever grant any one person absolute control over everything that happens in their lives. Before God emanated the material world, he was all-in-all, had complete control, was omniscient, omnipotent, and experienced everything that happened all at once. Nothing happened outside him, and in fact, nothing actually happened. Because there wasn't anything to happen. Because it was just ... God.

How boring! No wonder he emanated everything. No wonder he expressed himself in us human beings, a bunch of little creator gods all working together to create and experience the material world, each having to cooperate with everyone else in the overall group project.

But while we can't control everything absolutely, we always have choices that we can make that will change our experience of any situation. We have the ability to influence everything we experience, whether by meditating on a thing until we learn to see that even suffering is joy, or by deciding that we are miserable in a given situation and leaving it behind. There is always an escape, if you are willing to face the risks, challenges, and unpalatable potential outcomes.

There's no guarantee of success. You can try to make your world better, and end up making things worse. People sick of living under tyrants have tried to escape and wound up dying in prisons. Some have regretted that they didn't just put up with things when they weren't as bad, others feel fulfilled that at least they died trying to improve their lot.

Ultimately, it's up to us. What we decide to do with the situations at hand is entirely our choice. Everything not under our direct control is at least under our indirect influence.

And it doesn't matter what your current physical circumstances might be. Ghandi brought the British Empire to its knees. From a jail cell. He was able to do so because he had done a lot of work, taken advantage of a lot of opportunities, and expressed himself in ways that brought an Empire of rapacious white people under the authority of a skinny brown man who was under their power the whole time.

# Kings and Kingdoms

So now that we've gone over the basics, it's time to start weaving it together into the process at hand. We're here to make you into the King of your Kingdom.

The sphere of our experience, that is; everything that is under our direct control and indirect influence is our Kingdom. The fact that we control and influence our experience is what makes us the King of our Kingdom. In other words, you're a King. The absolute King of your world. You were born in the center of it, you will have more influence over your experiences than anyone else through the choices you make in life, and you alone will live with what you do long after those you influence have moved beyond your reach.

## Kings: What Makes You One

I've spelled it out in part all along the way, but the reason you're a King is because you are a child of God. You are a manifestation of God. You are made in God's image. The body you wear is the image of God. The spirit you are inside that body is the image of God. You are a direct descendent of God in our spiritual hierarchy.

What does that mean? I mean, think about it, you. Take a minute.

If your grandmother was pure Irish, and she married a man of pure Irish descent, wouldn't that make your mother or father pure Irish? Wouldn't that make you Irish as well?

Well guess what . . . Your original source was the First Father, the Prime Mover, the guy we nonchalantly call "God." Before you took form, you were recognized by the Planetary Governors as the Image of God, his child. When you poked your head through the material heavens, the Spiritus Mundi, the Spirit of the World saw you and made an animal form for you to inhabit in the form of the First Father, God, which you then descended into and took form. What's that mean?

You guessed it, you are descended from God.

Guess what race that makes you? Irish? Native American? Polish? African? White, Black, Mestizo, Asian?

Nope.

That makes you a . . .

wait for it . . .

wait for it . . .

That makes you *a god!*

Note that I said "a god." Not THE GOD. Although in a way it is true, you don't get to be the whole of all that is the eternal and unending Source of all that is, was, or ever will be as long as you're still in a manifested, individuated form. It would be rather convenient to have infinite power and stuff. And frankly, it is totally possible to have moments of complete and absolute power over everything, for a time. But that kind of power is a special thing, and we don't get to be there all the time.

But still, being a lowercase "g" god does make you pretty powerful. Have you ever read the Greek myths? There are all kinds of stories about the lives of the people who were descended from the gods. Hercules, Atalanta, Orpheus, Perseus, Jason—they all had something about them that made them more powerful than the average human. They were demi-gods, somewhere between the mortal and immortal, more than men, yet here for shorter periods than the gods. Sound familiar? Because that's you.

The Great Work is an alchemical method of refining base elements into a purified form. It takes lead and makes it into gold by a process of heat and chemical transformations. The process itself is a real chemical process. It isn't just a spiritual metaphor; it's a chemical formula that takes "minium," Latin for cinnabar (although more commonly used to refer to triplumbic tetraoxide, but also cinnabar in earlier texts), and turns it into vermillion, the dark red pigment sought after by the artists from ancient Rome to China and into Renaissance Europe. Vermillion was so valuable that having the formula to turn the red lead into vermillion was like being able to make pure gold. The alchemist who figured out how to do it without getting mercury poisoning had an income for life.

But it's more than that. It's also an alchemical allegory for the spiritual process we put ourselves through. We are the base matter, the prime material, that we treat. In our occult pursuits, we conjure the spirits, draw down powers, purifying us and cleansing us, improving our memories of the entities we are inside the material form. We get more power as we go along, because we are being transformed from the average, ignorant mortal to the fully aware, individual, incarnated god that we really are. It is a process of being introduced to our extended family members whose presence reminds us who we are and empowers us to be what we need to be.

That's why we spend so much time conjuring spirits in our rites. One of the most commonly used rites in modern ceremonial magic is the Lesser Banishing Ritual of the Pentagram. I am not a big fan of the use and representation of this rite amongst the hoi polloi, because it is not explained to be an actual conjuration ritual that results in the conjuration of the Four Angels of the Corners of the World, that is, the Four Kings of the Material Realms. More emphasis is put on the superfluous pentagrams traced than the actual conjuration of the Angelic kings. Nine out of ten practitioners of this rite will tell you it banishes all the energies of an area, and few of them will believe you when you tell them it's a conjuration rite.

But it is. The reason it "banishes energies" is because when you conjure the four angelic kings of the Elemental Realms, any of the terrestrial spirits of those elements are instantly going to be put in their proper places. The angels you call on are the Kings, and calling on them to help you out is a great way to make sure the mischievous underlings of their realms aren't bothering you or messing around with you during the next phase of your conjuration. They are also good to have on hand to assign spirits to materialize your desires. If you, you know, mention that to them. It helps to put it into words.

Conjuration rites are the key to my personal success and the main method of magic that I will be teaching the rest of my life in the flesh on the Earth. At least, it looks that way from here. If I stumble upon some magical mystical way to automatically enlighten people by thinking magic words at them, I'll be teaching that, I guarantee!

But in the meantime, conjuring spirits is the only method I've found provides you with the initiations, empowerments, training, and knowledge that we need to have to complete the spiritual Great Work. Being in the presence of the spirits of the Spheres is enough to initiate (which means "to begin") the changes in our spheres that make us the empowered creator-gods we actually are under the surface. It's a matter of harmonics and resonance. When I teach in public, I show a picture of an XKCD comic that explains resonance. Basically, when you pluck a properly tuned G-string in a guitar store, all the other properly tuned G-strings will vibrate as they react to the sound waves hitting them.

Likewise, when you conjure up the pure essential Intelligence or Archangel of the sphere of Saturn, the parts of you that received a portion of the powers of Saturn are going to start to vibrate. As the Saturn-aspects of you begin to vibrate, the things that block you from being able to manifest the forces of Saturn in your daily life begin to get knocked loose. This process builds with exposure—the more the Saturn parts of your sphere vibrate, the more crap gets shaken off, and pretty soon, you find yourself manifesting the forces of Saturn like a boss.

Note that this resonance with planetary forces is not always a particularly pleasant experience. You may have a lot of Venus-issues built up in your magician's sphere because, I don't know, your parents never loved themselves enough to love one another in a healthy way, or maybe the first person you ever loved laughed at you when you expressed your feelings and you shut down rather than being hurt again.

If that's the case, when the spirits of Venus start popping up, and the Venus-related aspects of your sphere start vibrating in resonance to the spirits' purity and power, the crap will get shaken off, and it will rise to the surface before it disappears. When it's gone, you will be a healthier person, able to direct the forces of the sphere of Venus into your life and the lives of those you love in your Kingdom in a righteous way. You'll be able to love and to be loved, and you'll be able to honor the feelings of others.

And the same is true of each of the spheres: whatever crap you have built up about receiving the blessings of Jupiter (I don't deserve to be blessed because I'm a bad, bad man), or the just application of the forces of Mars (fuck the police!), or the ability to take right action in a Solar leadership role (I'm not fit to tell others what to do), or any issues you have over commerce (Property is theft!/Socialism is welfare!), or the Lunar cycle of manifestation and un-manifestation of existence (it's not fair that what I want goes away!) will all get shaken out. Dealing with those issues can be painful, but only if you really try hard to hold on to the things that need to be let go.

If you're willing to lose everything you have to get something better, you will have no issues whatsoever. Believe me, I fully understand that there are situations in life that can seem to be "not so bad" or "worth putting up with" that you won't necessarily want to lose, things that you don't want to fall apart because you think you owe someone your temporary suffering for a some future reward, or for some mysterious greater good.

You're free to stay in that misery for as long as you want, but I guarantee that when you're willing to put everything you have, everything you *are*, on the altar and say, "take anything that is broken and make me into the awesome person I am meant to be," you will find that you are transformed into something amazing. Every bad situation you clung to in fear or out of a misplaced loyalty or sense of obligation will be replaced with something beautiful, healthy, and rewarding.

And you'll find an awesome secret. By receiving initiations and empowerments in the spheres above, we bring our Kingdom into harmony with the process of manifestation. Initiations release powers into our Kingdoms. The power flows like a liquid into our spheres. This power washes out blockages, and when it's complete, the powers are flowing stronger, clearer, with a vibrant potency, and we have established a current from the planetary sphere into our own sphere that we are free to wield as we see fit.

And here's the thing about "as we see fit." Some people get annoyed with me when I tell people this magical process is empowering and we can do whatever we want to with the power. They react, basically, out of fear. They look at the majority of the un-illuminated people around us, or perhaps it's at the dark desires of their own hearts, and say, "You can't tell people they can do whatever they want! Look at Hitler/Rapists/Charlie Manson! You're bad, bad, bad, and irresponsible, RO!"

Sigh . . . It's always an indicator to me that when people are proclaiming my irresponsibility in pointing out the inherent freedom and power of your basic incarnated human being that they have not been through the initiations I am talking about. If they had, they would understand some really essential things about initiations and empowerments.

As we go through the initiations we gain insight and ability, it's true, and yes, we gain power . . . but we also gain wisdom and understanding. We learn who we are as human beings; we learn what it means *to be human*. We see ourselves, all of us, every one of us, as manifestations of a divine and holy source, and we see how beautiful and wonderful that can be. We learn compassion, and control. We learn to separate our base desires that bring destruction and pain from the true desires that bring happiness and mutual satisfaction to all in our Kingdom.

We are transformed into benevolent, kind, compassionate, and powerful entities whose personal desires are aligned with the Good desires that benefit all humankind. It's just how it goes. The power comes with the ability and wisdom to use it righteously.

That doesn't mean we don't curse people who suck though. Just for the record. Sometimes we are white blood cells attacking diseased tissues that are destroying the host. And the only way we know when to curse is when we feel like it. So . . . don't think you'll always feel nice and kind and wonderful personally. You'll still get enraged by injustice, and you'll react accordingly. It will simply be in alignment with the Will of God. But let's talk about the power. Initiations provide an influx of power. Power is great, if it can be converted to Work. An engine takes the power of exploding chemicals and converts it to work. It channels an explosion into something useful. Electric motors do the same thing, converting electrical energy into mechanical energy so it can do work.

The process we go through in this book is the process of upgrading our engines so it can convert the spiritual energy into mechanical energy now. That's Mars, by the way, and the Sun, and Venus, and Mercury, and also the Moon.

The last few chapters have laid the foundation of the mystical aspects of the things we're going to be doing. We've gone over the mystical core of what we're doing (Magic to get the power, wisdom, and authority to be the Kings of our personal Worlds), why the magic works (because you're a divine being from a long line of divine beings), and how it works (by bringing the pure essences of our divine family members into resonant contact with our spheres to remind us who we are and to empower us to do our Wills upon the Earth).

In many occult books that I've read, the metaphysical aspects, the "belief system," was something I would skim over to get the key pieces in my mind to understand how the practical stuff was supposed to work, and then I'd start doing the magics, awwwww yeeeeeeeeaaaaaaaah . . . I expect people to do that here too. I wouldn't have learned the secret that I'm about to tell you if I hadn't done it that way myself, but really, the next sentences are the most important ones in this book:

Everything I just told you is the absolute applicable truth; you really are an immortal god walking around in a temporary flesh suit, and you are capable of creating your life in ways beyond your wildest imaginations because you are made in the image of a creator god, and that's what makes you *fucking awesome.*

Everything else I ever teach is going to be about that. I teach methods to get people to learn who they are, where they come from, and what they are capable of doing with that awesome power. That's it. I teach you to know yourself, to know what that means. It's pretty simple. You're a god. You do god stuff. 'Cause . . . that's what gods do.

I'll close out the mystical stuff here with a quote from the one author of occult information that you ever really need to read, if you've got the time: Heinrich Cornelius Agrippa. This is from his *Third Book of Occult Philosophy*, in chapter 36:

> *Whosoever therefore shall know himself, shall know all things in himself; especially he shall know God, according to whose Image he was made; he shall know the world, the resemblance of which he beareth; he shall know all creatures, with which he Symbolizeth; and what comfort he can have and obtain, from Stones, Plants, Animals, Elements, Heavens, from Spirits, Angels, and every thing, and how all things may be fitted for all things, in their time, place, order, measure, proportion and Harmony, and can draw and bring to himself, even as a Loadstone Iron.*

## Kingdoms: Really, It's All about Kingdom Maintenance

To recap, your personal Kingdom is your personal sphere. Anything that you can directly or indirectly control or influence is a part of your kingdom. Your car, your spouse/partner, your kids, your friends, your pets, your home, your job, your favorite bar, your liquor shelf—everything that you experience in your life at any given time is a part of your Kingdom. I talk about using the rites in this book to "establish your kingdom," but the truth is, you've already got a kingdom. The rites in this book just sort of help you understand what that means, while giving you a set of tools that you can use to manage your kingdom.

You have to manage your life like a King manages his Kingdom. Each of the planetary spheres represents a force, an aspect of existence that manifests in your life. Everything we experience is a manifestation of their forces mingled in varying proportions. The aspects of life that have more combative qualities fall primarily under the influence of Mars, while the aspects of life that have more to do with the procreative aspects of your world will fall under the influence of Venus.

Each of the planetary forces rules an aspect of your Kingdom too. By tapping into the forces of each of the planets, we can get the various parts of our kingdoms cleaned up that need to be cleaned up, or get things flowing that are stuck, or make contacts to get things we need. But before we can start Working on them, we need to really have a good, clean understanding of the current status of our kingdom. What King can rule who doesn't know the current events of their kingdom?

So . . .

How's your kingdom looking?

There are budgetary concerns to address, fundamental prosperity issues to understand and cultivate. Are you a wealthy and prosperous kingdom with plenty of resources and multiple revenue streams, or are things tight all over? Do the people in your kingdom have access to the basics of modern life with a little left over for fun, or are they struggling to make ends meet?

What about your military? Are your borders protected? Are you safe from invaders, or if it became necessary to invade, would you have the forces necessary to do so? You have to inspect your armed forces. Determine if you will be campaigning for more resources in the future, and determine whether your forces are strong enough to bring you conquest, or if they will be soundly thrashed, revealing to those who would harvest your crops for themselves a weak and vulnerable target.

And in that same vein, if you've been campaigning abroad to get more resources, make sure to check your defenses. Have your strategies for conquest left you exposed and vulnerable at home? Is your castle provisioned, are the stones strong, is there pure water available in case of a siege?

How do the people in your kingdom see you? Do they see you as their King, noble, just, and kind? Do they turn to you for fair and just resolution of their issues? Do they trust you to protect them, to provide for them, and to care for them in their times of need? Or are there hidden resentments, long-standing disputes, plots, and intrigues happening against you behind your back?

What does your Kingdom produce that is valuable to the people who live within its borders or valuable for trade with those in other kingdoms? How much can your kingdom produce with the resources you have available?

Are you over-utilizing portions of your kingdom, or under-utilizing others? How are relationships in your kingdom? Are there harmonies that make even difficult times easier to bear, or deep-seated rivalries and resentments that result in the poisoning of every attempt to make things better?

How is the *flow* of your kingdom? Are there inputs and outputs, does information flow into and out of your kingdom along established and predictable lines of well-maintained infrastructure? Are you taking part in commerce, in trade, in exchanges of value that leave you in a better position when the dust settles? Do you have an established network of friends, family, and co-workers that keep you apprised of opportunities as they arise, and do you pass on the opportunities that are best suited for others?

How are things manifesting in your Kingdom? Does the work you put forward result in the materialization of the things you've worked towards? Do you let things pass into the un-manifest realms without trying to cling to them when their time is done? Are the cycles of materialization recognized and worked with harmoniously by the people of your kingdom, and are there regular, predictable schedules of activity that can be depended on by those who rely on you and yours?

And lastly, how are your borders? Are you over-extended, and maybe need to contract your borders a bit because you just don't have the resources to support the needs at hand? Or is it time to consider expanding your borders to extend your reach, your resources, and your revenues?

In the following sections, we'll be discussing the ways the planetary forces manifest in a person's Kingdom. I've tried to reveal the mysteries of each sphere as it relates to a King, to give you the insight and understanding to utilize the forces in your personal management techniques. This information has helped me understand when and where to apply my attention and how to focus it to bring about the thing that I love the most, the thing that I think is perhaps the solution to all the personal and interpersonal problems in all the nations and kingdoms upon the Earth: joy.

# Jupiter

On April 14, 2011, I had the good fortune of falling in with an online resurgence of the Jupiter Cult. I don't pretend to understand what exactly happened, but through a sequence of rather extraordinary events, a couple of magicians decided to start a Gentleman's Club (that is open to all genders, oddly enough) dedicated to Jupiter. At least once a month, and weekly if possible, on the Day and Hour of Jupiter, we put on our formal apparel, smoke fine cigars, drink fine whiskey, and perform a ritual in honor of Jupiter.

The results of this little effort in the lives of the participants have been awesome, and I'm writing this booklet to provide you with access to the same kind of blessings we've been experiencing.

## Jupiter Magic Overview: Why Jupiter Magic is GOOD

The Sphere of Jupiter had, up until this event, been one of the least appreciated spheres in my particular application of the Great Work. Early in my magical transformation, I received a quick initiation into the Sphere of Jupiter, something that laid the foundation for the forces of Jupiter to manifest through my sphere and impact the world around me, and enough to provide a tentative relationship with the Spirits of Jupiter for use in my regular practice. And that was pretty much it.

The first Jupiter rite I did was modeled on the story of Israel Regardie's success. He did a Jupiter rite to get rich, and within a couple of weeks he was doing some massage therapy on one of his clients, and he got a hot stock tip. Regardie invested everything he had in the stock, and made a fortune. He was able to quit his day job and pursue occult practice and his writing full time.

That sounded exactly like what I needed, so I conjured up Sachiel and put in a request for wealth, riches, and prosperity. I promptly got a new job offer, and took it! And soon I was making *less* than I was before.

"What gives?" I asked Sachiel in a panic. Lowered income is not something I adapt to readily. In response I got images of ledgers, budgets, graphs, charts and stuff that looked like slides from a personal finance seminar. I also got a strong sense that the Intelligence of Jupiter wanted me to learn how to properly manage my resources so I could fulfill my responsibilities as a good steward.

That didn't go over so well in the Rufus Opus sphere of magical practice.

So, thanking Sachiel for his work, I did what any self-respecting beginner magician who had just figured out that spirits are real and conjure magic works *would* do: I conjured up a demon for some fast cash.

And it came, and I promptly forgot all about Jupiter.

Demon magic tends to end badly, and in retrospect . . . well, I wish I had listened to Sachiel in the first place years ago.

But after that, I kind of held a little tiny bit of a grudge. That experience colored my understanding of Jupiter from that day on, and I thought the Tzedeq (Jupiter in Hebrew is Tzedeq, by the way) spirits were a bunch of lawyer/accountant types. They would appear in grey suits wearing spectacles and carrying briefcases in my conjure rites, and I sort of shelved Jupiter and his spirits. I would go there to get insight on behalf of my clients, but I never really asked for much from them.

Then the Gentlemen for Jupiter mystery cult was founded, and I participated in the founding day's Work. That ritual was not a request for anything in particular, and was primarily intended to be a formal observation of the forces of Jupiter. What I got was far beyond what I expected!

I was blessed with a Vision of the Grace of Jupiter. This has fundamentally changed the way I look at life. I received instruction and guidance, and a Jupiter Empowerment that has influenced everything I've touched since then. And that's just the spiritual revelations.

There have been material and financial revelations of equal value too, directly and indirectly. In one week, I was inspired to write up two publications for sale and distribution through my site, which brought in a decent income, and I sold four Jupiter Talismans for $500. Not only that, I got out of over $75,000 in potential fines and penalties on taxes, to get a refund of a few grand on top of that, all because an IRS agent had mercy and extended grace to me. And the really cool part is that I got to see it happening, like through the eyes of Jove or something, see it coming down through the spheres and into my experienced reality. Good times!

Jupiter magic is *good* magic. They don't call Jupiter the Greater Benefic for nothing! Jupiter is expansion, growth. It is all things good. It is fun. It is power, authority, but the good sides of that. It is blessing. It is the righteous smiting of your enemies for fun and good result, like in a good-natured bar brawl where you teach someone it's not nice to call your date a bitch or a whore, or the exuberance shown in *Fight Club*. It is profit, profit through expanded opportunity. It is joy, Joy with a capital "J." It is health also; the images of Jupiter include a robust red-faced man laughing. It is jolly, like Santa. It is increase, prosperity, the fullness of life itself.

And it's responsible with all this goodness, not all extremely hedonistic, like the dark side of Venus/Netzach. It can hold its liquor and still take care of the State better than a Russian prime minister.

# GRACE

There's a reason Chesed, the sphere associated with Jupiter on the Tree of Life is translated as Grace in English. Grace is a mixture of forgiveness and aid. It's like when you've done something wrong, and you're guilty of doing it, and you know it, and you're expecting the fitting punishment that you acknowledge you deserve, and instead of getting that, you get pardoned, forgiven, and a million dollars as well, with the admonition to do better this time around. It's not something you earn either; it's not a reward for REALLY being sorry or anything. It's just grace. A free gift for you to enjoy instead of any punishment you may deserve.

That's the key to the core of Christianity, by the way, the thing that freed Martin Luther that so many modern, so-called Christians just don't get. Grace. Martin Luther's revelation came as he trudged up a bazillion steps on bleeding knees meditating on the scriptures. Quick note here: Martin Luther was fucked UP. Just sayin'.

But his revelation was all about one scripture in particular:

> *For by grace you have been saved through faith; and that not of yourselves, it is the gift of God; not as a result of works, so that no one may boast.*

By Grace you have been saved. I don't want to get into soteriology and how the Christians adapted and adopted the neo-platonic ideas of Henosis into their beliefs over the last couple of thousand years, but let's just say Luther's revelation is spot on from the perspective of Hermetics.

Luther labored under the delusion that his "sin" kept him separate from God, even though the version of scripture he got his hands on was pretty clear. After putting himself through personal hell, he realized the clear truth: salvation, the return to being a friend and co-worker with the Source of all we are, is something we can just have *because it's a gift*. He realized no matter how bad he thought he was, no matter what the Church or any other human told him, God thought Luther was so freaking awesome that he just GAVE HIM forgiveness for any sleights. Not only that, he also gave him empowerment to change the entire world. And he did, too.

Grace is the love of God towards all humankind, and more than that, it's his desire to be with us, to exalt us as his favored child within his kingdom. He wants us to be co-creators and maintainers of existence, and to hang out with him and talk to him about how cool it is, right?

Yeah . . . I don't know whether you're up for hearing a conversation between me and God, but basically, a lot of the time, it goes like this . . .

"Hey God, this is awesome; have you seen this shit?"

"Yes. I have."

"Freakin' amazing, man! Great Idea!"

"I know, right!?"

And then we laugh and get back to enjoying the moment.

And it's totally cool. Mutual enjoyment. *Divine* mutual enjoyment. It's a highly mystical concept, usually buried under layers and layers of initiation and other forms of bullshit, because it's really not as mystical-seeming as some of the more flabbergasting zen koans might appear to the un-illuminated.

But that's the whole point of Grace and salvation: it's all a big "C'mere, you!" from a really happy and proud Father who doesn't give a shit what you think you did wrong; he's just eager to get on to sharing the family business with you. Because he knows it is what will ultimately make you the happiest.

And honestly, there is nothing you will ever do that will feel as good as the day you step into your role, accept your responsibility, and start gathering the enormous powers it really takes to do all the things you can do as a magician called to magic. . . .

Just a second. Real quick: a magician is someone called to do magic to create and maintain their world. That's it, pretty much. Magicians are the ones who can't help but be attracted to the occult despite their upbringing, or despite their secular humanist views, or despite their rational skeptical doubts. They're the ones who can't explain the passion for this weird shit any more than a non-believer can, but nevertheless must feed that insatiable quest for knowledge, experience, and right action.

So if that describes you, congratulations, you're called to magic. And as magicians called to magic, you really were created to do what the Emerald Tablet says, to rise through the heavens, to return to the earth in power, and by this create the world. Until you start doing that, nothing will satisfy you, and the flip side of that is that as soon as you start doing that, you'll feel it in your bones; you will have taken the right step, done the right thing. As cliché as it sounds, you will be doing exactly what you were made to do, and you'll know it and love it.

And that's grace. 'Twas grace that brought you here. The power of Jupiter, the forces of him drawing you to him so you can experience more of him, and thus be more of you. I'm not saying Jupiter is the First Father; I'm saying his planet is a gateway to experience the Grace aspect of his sphere in your life, in a highly personal way.

## Applied Grace

Grace has this unique aspect to it that I keep learning about. I've learned it, and integrated it, and known it, but then I learn more about it, and then I feel like I barely know anything about it at all. There's always something new and deeper and more meaningful and more useful in magic to find.

Grace grows by being given away. When you receive that blessing from Jupiter, and you in turn pass on a blessing to others, you are able to receive more blessing. It's like a current. If you try to take all the blessings of Jupiter and keep them for yourself to make you personally happy, you've put a closed sphere at the bottom of a tube that has fluid flowing into it. When the sphere is full and the pressure in the sphere reaches equilibrium, no more fluid will flow. But you put a spigot on that sphere, let the fluid flow out, and all of a sudden you've got a current.

The Grace of the sphere of Jupiter never runs out. By passing it along, you become a channel for Grace, and on its way through you from on High, it will manifest in your life. You give charity, and you have more charity to give.

So if you do a Jupiter rite and then get some cash, give some cash to the next person you see. Don't judge them if they're poor, drunk, or homeless; forgive and reward with more than they asked for. What you give will come back to you quickly.[1]

If you get a debt forgiven, forgive a debt someone owes you. If you learn something new, teach someone something new. Pass it on, and don't be afraid to make a profit on it, because that's part of this too. Prosperity. Necessary wealth. You're a King in the sphere of Jupiter, and a Kingdom needs funds.

## Authority: Divinely Right Rulership

Which brings us to another aspect of Jupiter that I want to try to put into words. Right Rulership.

When I received this latest initiation into Jupiter, I got this Vision, see. There was Jupiter pouring out his graces into my sphere, and I saw that mechanically, the more I passed on, the more I had capacity for, and that the Jupiter Current widened itself in my sphere as it passed through, letting me put even more through.

But I also saw myself in relation to others in my life. I saw that, from my perspective, I'm the center of my universe, and in spite of fate or destiny, it seems to us in the flesh that we are the masters of our fate. I've never really understood that, because our ignorance of the future leaves us stuck in agnosis over the whole free will vs. fate issue.

But for all intents and purposes, we are little Kings and Queens of our own little Kingdoms. We have roles and responsibilities to fulfill, and there are those in our lives who depend on us for their own survival and happiness. We have social obligations and reap social rewards. We are intricately connected to everything and everyone we interact with, and we play really big roles in the daily lives of those we interact with, no matter what we might think. And as magicians who are called to create and maintain the world, we have a lot of freaking power at our fingertips. The more wisdom and experience we get, the more we understand how to use this power we have. The more we can be trusted with, the more we get, and the more things there are to take care of. It's a cycle I've understood for a while, but Jupiter's role in all this eluded me.

---

[1] Don't be stupid though; foolish squandering of Jupiter's resources will not be rewarded with more resources. Mars and the Sun are good spheres to visit after a Jupiter rite to find the right balance in your Grace bestowing activities.

Jupiter provides the *divine authority to rule well*. Kings are kings because they are of noble blood. Nobility is finer stuff than the common stuff, or at least that's the theory. We know better in our egalitarian world, that genetics alone does not make a person a good leader. There has to be a combination of sovereignty, authority, an understanding of justice, fairness, and the role of law, and the power to overcome evil when we see it, but there also has to be grace in order to rule well.

The nobility used to be called "Your Grace" by people under them. I think that's a direct reference to this Jovial quality that makes a Ruler a Good Ruler. The ability to forgive and reward when there's something of merit in the recipient.

In my life this manifests as patience, of all things. Turning my attention and love to those who need them. In business it's helping others in a similar craft, giving them a leg up, supporting their services. It takes discernment to know when to be gracious, and when you're slipping into foolishness, but solid work with all the spheres will keep you balanced.

## Applied Right Rulership

What kind of King are you? How's life in your kingdom for those who share it? How much authority have you got over your situation? I guarantee, you can have more if you start by taking responsibility, and doing the right thing.

And the right thing is not always clear, but you go with what you feel, what your intuition tells you. Have confidence in it; see where it leads. If it leads you astray at first, don't panic. It gets better. Mistakes suck, but you're going to make them. You might as well learn from them. Pretty soon, you'll find you do the right thing automatically. And cliché as it may sound, you'll find that you're making the world a better place in the process.

## Oh yeah, the Power

I hesitate to mention this, but it's kind of something you'll figure out on your own anyway, and I wouldn't want it to surprise you.

When you do this ritual, you're going to become more powerful. You'll be able to do more things, to influence more things. You'll have authority over aspects of your life you didn't have before. You'll be able to help more people than you imagined. Of course, on the flip side, you'll also be able to hurt more people than ever before, so you know, be careful.

There's a buzz I got after doing the rite. When I became aware of it, I wasn't paying much attention to it, as it's not abnormal to catch a buzz from magic. It usually fades away as you integrate the forces of the sphere, or it dissipates. You might have a problem getting to sleep after a rite, but then it fades and it's not that big of a deal.

This kept building over three days. By the height of it, I was a manic Jovial fiend, in a good way.

I think.

I don't think I bit anyone's head off, or struck down anyone with flaming lightning bolts, but I was consumed with expansive powers.

And by expansive, I mean everything I turned my attention to, everything I looked at, I could see prospering. From the formation of the Gents to my writing project, to the accomplishment of the Great Work itself, I could see it all happening, unfolding in an unstoppable series of events that would make the world . . . a better place.

I finished three major writing projects in a few short days, things I'd been working on and planning came first, and then finished up a chap-book based on my Jupiter Work. I couldn't resist writing it any more than I could resist breathing.

I got a ton of crap done at work too, and a lot of personal finance business cleaned up in a few short days. And I made a lot of money too. Money is good.

## The Danger

Of course, there are dangers. The danger of Jupiter power released into your sphere is that it will bring expansion, and you won't deal with it. You've got to get that shit under control right away. Harness it before it dissipates; get it flowing like a siphon so it creates suction and draws more down. Jupiter will give, and give, and give if it gets a chance to, but if your Kingdom doesn't have the infrastructure in place to handle that kind of blessing, it will wash everything away in a flood of biblical proportions.

## Mars

By passing through the Gate of Jupiter, you receive an anointing. You become a King, the ruler of your Kingdom. Your Kingdom is your sphere of sensation, everything you interact with around you. You are the ruler of that kingdom, and with that rulership comes all the responsibilities a King must face.

To meet one's responsibilities, one must rule their kingdom well. One obvious aspect of rulership is the establishment and following of Rules. The use of Law. Mars is the sphere of the Law, and it is the sphere immediately below Jupiter on the Chain of Manifestation.

It makes sense, doesn't it? When you receive the anointing of Kingship in Jupiter, you're a King by divine declaration. You have the divine right to rule your kingdom. You're a newly appointed King.

The first thing a newly appointed King needs to do is to get a really good understanding of his kingdom. Hopefully in real life, our political and temporal rulers spend a lot more time learning about their kingdom before they actually take on their role as Ruler, but I gave up believing in hope in politics sometime after my first Lunar initiation, when I learned to see through glamour, illusion, and the fundamental lies people present on their outermost forms.

For our purposes, we'll assume the King has no clue about anything, that circumstances and fate have thrust a kingdom onto him, knowing he is the man for the job. And he is, otherwise the Authorities wouldn't have made him King, right? So he's got the capacity to be a good King, singled out by God Jehovah Jove Jupiter himself.

But he's got to figure out the current status of the Kingdom before he can start making good decisions as the leader. You've got to take a similar inventory of your Kingdom to begin to understand the rules you'll need to follow to make your kingdom thrive.

In previous sections, we talked about taking an inventory of your kingdom in its current state. When you have taken a look at how the different spheres are manifesting in your life right now, before you begin doing the Work, you'll find yourself with a pretty comprehensive understanding of what you need to work on. You'll identify different aspects of your Kingdom that need to be improved.

Write this stuff down. Make a list. Then take a look at the list and decide what is most important, what needs your attention first, second, third, etc. When you prioritize this list of things to do, you find that, voila, you've got yourself the basics of a plan, a set of steps you have to take to get your kingdom where you want it to be.

The successful completion of each item on your list is your goal. If solving our problems were simple, we'd have done it already. There are things we do instead of solving our problems. This is where rules come into play, and are valuable. To get from wherever you are currently to the goal, you will need to identify the rules that you'll have to follow in order to get from here to there.

## Rules and Governance: the Art of Kingship

Rules can be tricky. I was raised to fear "The Law." Rules and laws and regulations and standards had to be kept to avoid punishment. It was in my religion, it was in my secular education, it was in my jobs from the beginning of my career to the present day. Rules, obeying the rules is important; it keeps you out of trouble.

But rules took on a different meaning when I started going through the initiations and doing the magic of the Hermetic Great Work. I stopped seeing them as threats of punishment, and started seeing that they were there to help. The rules are set up to guide, not to command. They mark the boundaries, and serve as warnings. They aren't to be feared or resented; they are to be respected and used as advice to get ahead and reap the rewards of the Jupiter blessing.

Rules are like guard rails on the side of the mountain highways; they don't really protect you from death if you hit them straight on, but they do wake you up if you're falling asleep. And they provide a good reference for your boundaries.

And that's how a Jupiter King rules their Kingdom, by establishing guidelines, by identifying the ways they need to behave in order to accomplish their goals. They don't set up the Rules as the punisher; they set them up as the assistants, the aids towards the goal. And they don't punish themselves for failing. Jupiter is about Grace, forgiveness. You don't need to be all harsh to get back on course; you just need to apply a little self-discipline and return to the path between the guidelines.

Mars helps provide that level of self-discipline. Receiving the initiation that comes from this rite will aid in the gentle application of discipline. Remember that "Discipline" comes from the Latin root word "discipulus," or student. That's where the word "disciple" comes from too.

When you discipline yourself, you are making yourself a student, teaching yourself the right way to behave to get what you want. How do you learn best, through Spartan severity, or through patient explanations and redirection? I'm somewhere in between, personally. Find the right balance for yourself; seek it through Mars.

## The Art of War

Now, rulership through rule-making isn't the primary function of Martial magic. It's the first thing that sprang to mind after passing through the Gate of Jupiter, but it helps the Anointed King rule their kingdom in other ways as well.

When you did your inventory, one of the things I mentioned was checking your defenses and the status of your armed forces. This is a martial trait that you can address from the Gate of Mars.

The first things to fix up are your defenses. Most of us do not suffer from constant magical, psychic, or even alien attack. Most of us live relatively normal, quiet, peaceful lives . . . but you're reading a pretty advanced occult book right now, and you're preparing to do some advanced magic. Chances are pretty good that this is not the first time you've been exposed to the occult. Your personal circles and social contacts are more likely to include pagans, occultists, magicians, and esoteric lodge members than the average Joe and Jane Sixpack.

As a result, every once in a while, some magician might take something we say out of context, or maybe some ex-lover will try to get us back, or get back at us, or their latest significant other may have it in for us and may try to curse us because we dared to have ever been of interest to their beloved, and rather than just sticking to mundane normal ways of taking out their aggressions, they will resort to magical attack. Fortunately for most of us, these types are usually pretty powerless, and while their negativity may wash over us, it doesn't linger.

For the kinds of normal life threats we face, standard hedges of protection are sufficient. An angelic hedge of protection around your kingdom is enough to keep most trespassers out. Putting one up is as simple as asking the Intelligence of the sphere to place a hedge of protection around your sphere, to keep out things that would harm you or anyone in your kingdom.

Sometimes we happen to piss off the wrong person though. A snide comment on an occult web site is often enough to draw down the unmitigated wrath of an egotistical madman with access to nefarious spirits. The jilted lover may hire a professional to get you back, or their latest significant other may do the same. We also attract undesirables of the spirit realms on occasion as we go about our magical activities, especially when we're first starting out and haven't figured out which neighborhoods we shouldn't enter after dark without an armed guard. Things find us, follow us home, and set about destroying the things we hold dear.

Having a good set of defenses is imperative. Hopefully you've inspected what your sphere looks like as far as defenses go. Do you have a guardian spirit or spirits that protect you from the occasional misstep? Have you talked to them about how you want to be defended?

If you're one of those "Shields up, Mr. Sulu" types who direct energy fields with the power of their mind, have you checked the strength of your shields against an actual practitioner of magic? I've met some energy field manipulators with really good shielding capabilities, but most of the folks making loud and vociferous claims of their mental astral warrior powers I've seen don't have shit. One fellow who managed to annoy me had me expecting demonic guardians and impenetrable black ice protecting his astral temple, and when I got there a simple "Be not" encouragement turned his fortress to dust. That revealed the caliber of adversary I had attracted, and embarrassed me into moving right along.

One thing I believe firmly is that one should always have worthy enemies.

But take a few kicks at your defenses. Could they keep you safe from someone as skilled as you are? With the resources at your disposal, how long could someone else defend themselves from you? Are you comfortable living like that?

And as many have said, the best defense is a good offense. In the time of King David, it was the standard practice in the spring for the men to leave their city and go to war. The one time David didn't go out with his troops, he ended up hooking up with Bathsheba, and things got . . . ill. Like when the Fisher King of the Grail legend was wounded and the land fell to ruin, reflecting his malady.

If he'd just gone to war when it was time to go to war instead of hanging out in the city with the women and children, he wouldn't have had to murder Bathsheba's husband to hide the fact that he'd gotten her pregnant.

In other words, there is a time for war. War comes to us all in its season. Will you have it show up at your door, or will you go out and find it on your own terms?

Practically speaking, the Martial Forces are your armed forces. Defense and offense. I know most of us, myself included, do not think of ourselves as being very martial by nature in this day and age. That said, a lot of my business clients are totally warriors on the capitalist field. Some of the strongest Mars talismans I've made have gone to very successful businessmen around the globe.

But the rest of us are mostly the "I'll defend myself if I have to, but I don't go to bars looking to get in a fight" types. Thinking in martial terms about our lives is uncomfortable. I happen to love peace, and believe it is the state most people should exist in. Peace is better, you know? I turn the other cheek when I can.

But to be a proper King, you can't just put your head in the ground and pretend there is no such thing as war. It's coming, and it's coming for you personally. You will have to fight for something, something you need to have, or something you already have that someone wants to take from you. Sooner or later it happens to everyone. Having a well-trained and well-developed armed force and security system is important.

And I'm not talking all about astral magic here, either, or magical warfare. I'm talking about how you forgot to pay a ticket and you got pulled over driving on a suspended license and now you've got to go to court. Or you're up for a promotion at work, and two others are up for it too, and they've got degrees in the subject and all you've got is some related experience. Or Second Wife is trying to secure your ex-husband, so she's pulling the "I'm going to make you look like a bad mother and take your kids in the courts so I can show your ex how much better at being a woman I am than you, at least until I have kids of my own" game. You know that game if you're over thirty. Either it's happened to you, or one of your friends or co-workers. If you're under thirty—ha ha!—guess what joys YOU get to look forward to?

Point is, you've got to fight sooner or later, and Mars is where you get the skills, training, troops, and defense reinforcement you're going to need. Walking through the Gate of Mars is the first step. The next step is asking the Intelligences and Spirits of the sphere of Mars to teach you what you need to do, to make it so clear even you can understand it regardless of your ability to sense the spirit realm and its lessons.

Listen to them. Follow those opportunities of a martial nature that arise. Buy that Sun Tzu book, and *The Prince*. Read them. Implement them as you see fit in your sphere. Take care of your kingdom—it's your job.

And when the inevitable warfare breaks out in your sphere, you'll have options available because you've been through the Gate, and you've established a relationship with the spirits of the sphere. Call up Kammael in times of trouble, and get him to assign a battalion of troops to fight for you, to defend you and yours, and to attack those who stand against you. For some situations, you'll need a temporary familiar spirit to work with, and you can get one assigned to you through Kammael. After conjuring him, request the assistant, and get his name and seal. Work with this spirit to develop a strategy, and set him to sniping key targets, or designing pitfalls and deadly defenses.

Do not let Mars take over, though. Don't lose sight of the Grace of Jupiter, whence comes your anointing. Take what is yours, but be just. And remember always, the main aim of War is to bring Peace. The Orphic hymn to Mars ends not on the note of bloody warfare that exemplifies the martial spirit, but instead with a request for peace. Mars is bloodthirsty, but when victorious, he returns the weapons to the Earth from which they were made, and turns to wine and women to cool his fire. He is passion in peace as well as in war.

# The Sun

After we've received the Kingdom and the anointing, and we've established the rules and protected our kingdom, we have to get down to the actual business of ruling our kingdom. Everything else up to this point has been the initiatory steps of getting the kingdom established and sustainable. Now we begin to take action, to make the right decisions, and maneuver through our circumstances to change or create the world as we see fit.

In the sphere of the Sun, we project the divine right to rule our kingdom into the manifest world around us. It is the sphere of leadership, the sphere of nobility. Here the *anointing of the kingship* crystallizes and is projected into our kingdom.

The Sun is the sphere through which the powers of the heavens above (Mars, Jupiter, and Saturn) are channeled into the spheres below. As the sun in our galaxy is the raw food stuff of life on Earth, so also the sphere of the Sun projects the essential powers we need to sustain all aspects of life within our kingdom. As the sunlight can be harnessed to provide nearly unlimited energy to our culture, so also the power of the sphere of the Sun can be tapped to provide the powers we need to keep our lives running.

The Sun is also the source of light in our galaxy, and light is a powerful force. Light dispels shadows, reveals things in their true form. Light burns things that dwell in shadow, destroys the things that dwell deep beneath the Earth and sea. If you've seen a worm dried on sunny concrete, you know what I'm talking about. The Solar sphere has a similar effect on the creepy things of the supernatural underworld when they go beyond their assigned boundaries. Don't get me wrong: I greatly appreciate the value of Underworld entities. They are every bit as necessary and useful as worms and other underworld, nocturnal, or creeping creatures are to life on earth.

But you don't want worms and slugs in your house.

The Sun is also the sphere of empowerment. The solar initiation has long been associated with attaining Knowledge and Conversation with the Holy Guardian Angel (K&CHGA). The passage through the sphere of the Sun is symbolized by the crucifixion of Christ, in that it usually comes with a great deal of pain that destroys you, only to bring you back to life again with expanded power and authority. The Solar initiation provides the heat of the alchemical Great Work, transforming the Prima Materia into the Philosopher's Stone.

As kings, the Solar sphere represents how we push the powers we received in Jupiter out to our kingdoms. It's the actual rulership that we do in our life that leads to the accomplishment of our goals. In Mars we made the rules; in the Sun we implement them.

In this way, the sphere of the Sun manifests sort of like your upper middle management of a corporation. The Vice Presidents are responsible for projecting down to the supervisors the goals and overall vision of the CEO up in Jupiter. They are responsible for projecting the corporate policies established in Mars. At the same time, they have to listen to those who report to them, review the reports, and make sure things are going according to plan.

It is a sphere that comes with great blessing and power, but also great responsibility.

## Feeding the Kingdom

One of the things that cracks me up about this whole Great Work thing is the "Now What" phase of the Great Work. In the early stages, it's pretty simple to figure out what we're supposed to be doing with magic. Conjure the elementals and work with them to get initiation into the forces that make up the world, conjure the spirits of the celestial spheres to get initiation and transform into more enlightened and empowered magicians, perform Liber Samekh or the Abramelin rite to get K&CHGA. We have clear goals, and somewhat clear methodologies that can be followed up to a point, but then we hit the Solar Initiation of K&CHGA, and the great magical question we all face is, "Now what?"

There is this idea in the modern occult realm that attaining K&CHGA is the same as attaining Enlightenment, and that as soon as you get to that point, you will just know what to do, automatically, and everything will be easy, and everything will just make sense.

## The Sun

In reality, when you reach K&CHGA, you become a very powerful magician with access to greater potentials and a much wider spectrum of tools. You get access to aspects of Deity that you weren't equipped to comprehend before. You get access to instruction, wisdom, and authority that make it possible to be a great magician-king of your world. But you don't get an instruction book. It doesn't tell you what to do now that you're a fully equipped powerful force of creation. You still have to figure that out on your own.

The Sun is the sphere of doing. It equips you to do things better. Whether you are doing what it takes to get rich, or to raise a family, manage a business, or whatever it is you're doing, the things you do are the way you project your rulership of your kingdom into your life.

You get an idea, and you go do it. You do what it takes to make your idea manifest. You project it into being by making it happen, by your actions.

You ever look at the Sun card in the Tarot deck? See those happy kids having fun in the sun? That's what they did. They got an idea that seemed like fun and they did it. They acted on it, and that's why they're happy. They are doing what they want to do, and it's fun.

What are you going to do? What do you want to do? Most people want to be rich and live a life of luxury. That's totally fine, honestly. There's nothing wrong with that at all. How will you project that into being if that's your goal?

The answers are usually simple, but enacting them is hard. Wealth is easy; you work hard, earn a lot, and live like a pauper. Sock as much away in an interest bearing account as possible. When you make enough on interest each month to pay for it, hire someone to invest wisely and increase the interest. After a while, you'll be really rich.

I spent time in a homeless shelter in my misspent youth, and one of the guys there with me was doing day labor as a carpenter. He'd gotten out of jail a few months before, and had nothing to start with. He lived and showered at the shelter, and went straight to work in the morning. At night he'd cash his day's pay and put it in the bank. Then he went to bed. In a few months, he'd managed to save up six grand, and had lined up a full time job that didn't give a shit about his criminal record because they could see he worked his ass off and showed up on time. Last I saw of him, he was putting his down payment on an apartment and a car.

There's no magic there, you know? It's a simple equation. Work over time earns money, and he spent next to nothing. It was hard, and he was exhausted at the end of each day, but he did it and reaped the reward.

I'm not telling you to go be a day laborer and live in a shelter to get rich. I'm pointing out that there are simple solutions to complicated problems if you're willing to do it. Around Christmas, I needed extra money, so I delivered pizzas. I made an extra $800 a month. It sucked for a few months, and motivated me to get my side revenue streams flowing a little stronger, but it was a simple solution to an immediate need.

Immediate needs require immediate responses. When you're hit with a huge, budget-crushing, unplanned expense that's going to screw your regularly scheduled payments for food, shelter, and clothing, you have an immediate need. It's not the time to start getting a new business off the ground. It's time to get some cash flow now. Fix the problem, plug the hole, and then start making your plans that will keep you from ending up in a similar solution in the future.

That's what the Solar gate empowers, the ability to act, and to make the right actions to address the needs of your kingdom. It rules the manifestation of your daily activities that support the kingdom.

When you did the gate of Mars, you took stock of your kingdom and identified the goals you aim to accomplish within your Kingdom. This should become your list of activities in your daily life. Each day you should be doing some solid activity between dawn and dusk that gets you closer to your goals.

If your goals are to earn more money, the activity should be either gaining the training or education you need to improve your skills, or applying for jobs that pay more for what you already know, or developing your product line to sell on your internet site that you've talked about in your blog.

Money's an easy example that most people can understand, which is why I keep talking about making it, but it's not all about money. It's all about getting what you want, accomplishing your goals, managing your resources and your time in a way to accomplish something that makes your personal world a better place.

If you're still stuck trying to figure out what you're supposed to be doing, take another look at the inventory and status report of your kingdom. You should have a pretty good understanding of the things that are going on in your life.

These things are the best indicators of what you should be doing. The job you already have, the responsibilities you already have to meet—these are what should be getting your attention first. How did you get into your current situation? What was the series of events that led to this? Most importantly, assess whether or not what you're doing, what you have, or where you're at in life is where you really want to be. If it's not, in any aspect, then guess what you should be doing? You should be identifying the steps to leave the situation you're in and to create the situation you desire ... and then you should be doing those things.

When you go through the Gate of the Sun, you will receive a great deal of power. Use the power you have received to accomplish your goals in each of the situations of your life that already exist. Improve relationships, do the tasks assigned, clean up those legal or financial issues, do the homework for that college course. Look around at the things that have popped up in your life since you've done the Jupiter Gate ritual. These opportunities are what you're supposed to be doing.

Whatever your hands can touch are really good indicators of "What next?" Do the things that are on your list, and do them well.

If you don't like them, change them, make plans and take steps. As you do so, you will be doing the things you are supposed to do as King.

## INTO THE LIGHT, I COMMAND YOU

In the Hermetic beliefs, the reason other spirits in the universe work with us, respect us, and love us is because we are made in the image of the First Father. They take one look at us, and because we remind them of God, we get all kinds of special treatment. The first Man received the power of each sphere to create as he descended through the spheres because he wanted to create, like God, and they wanted to help him, to teach him, to equip him to create out of love. It's like friends of your parents that see you and want to help you because they love your folks.

The authority over spirits, that is, the right to be able to perform an exorcism comes primarily from Jupiter, in my opinion.[2] When you were made a King, you were granted a measure of authority over all things that manifest. But that's just potential power there; it's not activated or directed until you reach the Sphere of the Sun.

---

[2] That's my "informed opinion," based on research and experience in the spirit realms. However, it's a theory, and if things happen to change my opinion, I will change the theory, and you should keep that in mind when I'm telling you what I think. I'm not a canon law dispenser; I'm just an observer and active participant in this creation thing.

In the Stele of Jehu, the foundational rite of Crowley's Liber Samekh, there's a section Crowley calls "the Rubric." In it, you say to the spirit, "Hear me and make every spell and scourge of man obedient unto me." There's more to it, but that's the important part here. That's what the power of the Sun does for you, and that's the part of this piece of initiation I'm talking about.

Michael the Archangel is the angel of the Sun in the system I use.[3] In many images, Michael is shown defeating a dragon or serpent, representing Satan. In the book of Revelations in the Bible, Michael is the one who throws Satan down from the heavens to the Earth. This symbolizes the power of the Sun over spirits of affliction.

Spirits of affliction exist. In the Corpus Hermetica, we learn that the "evil daimons" are sent to the impious to draw them closer to God. The idea is that with *some people*,[4] the only time they'll turn to their Immortal Source for help and assistance is when their life is shit. So God, to draw you to him, ruins your life.

Kinda shitty, in my opinion.

I do not believe that every bad thing that happens to me is God afflicting me to draw me closer to him. Sometimes it's just "shit happens." I also do not believe that every bad thing that happens to a person is happening because some evil spirit is accosting them.

There was a time when I didn't believe anyone was ever really demonized. I thought it was all in their heads. I thought bad shit happened to people usually because they didn't do what it takes to make things good in their lives. In other words, I believed if you're suffering it's all your fault. The natural consequence of bad decisions or ignorant actions is suffering, I thought, and it doesn't take a demon to bring that about any more than it takes a spirit to apply gravity to a person to keep them on the ground.

Then I started doing magic, and discovered there really are demons, and they really do bring afflictions against people. Whether it's on purpose by God's will to get you to call on him for help or not, I don't know. Regardless of whether that's the case or not, I do know that calling on God (doing magic to work with God or his manifest assistants) when you're dealing with a true

---

[3] In other systems, he's in Mercury, while Raphael is in the Sun. Raphael means "healing of God," and that's Mercury in my experience. Michael means "who is like God," and that is a Mystery, but is best manifested in the Sphere of the Sun, in my opinion.

[4] Not me, of course.

# The Sun

spiritual attack eliminates the spiritual attack. So it doesn't really matter why it happened as long as there's a way to make it stop.

I've also learned that people are afflicted by demons a lot more than I used to think they were. When I opened shop and started doing magic for clients, I expected to find that most people who thought they were demonized were just delusional. Then I started doing the divinations and found whole networks of tribes of evil spirits who really do make people's lives suck.

At some point, you will have to deal with malicious spirits. I have a lot of theories about who they are and why they manifest based on my work with them in the past and present, but the theories change frequently as different data comes in, so I won't get into any current interpretations. Generally speaking, it's sufficient to know that sooner or later you'll have to deal with malicious spirits, and the best possible way to do so is through the Sun.

In Mars we created and strengthened our defenses. We also posted guards. Sometimes we get attacked in ways we don't expect, sometimes we open ourselves up to it through our actions, and sometimes we even call up a spirit, let it past our defenses, only to have it end up attacking us. While you could go to Mars to get more troops, or you could go to Saturn to bind the attacker, I find that what works best when you find yourself in a fight with a malicious spirit is a quick blast of Solar power.

Most afflicting spirits can't stand the Sunlight, and will flee immediately when you start conjuring Michael the Archangel to bring the forces of the Sun to bear. Others will have to be chased out by Michael or another solar spirit. Regardless, the Solar power has the immediate effect of stopping the attack right now.

It does not automatically make the spirit go away for good. Malicious spirits are like underground things, grubs and worms, or those fish in the deep trenches of the sea that spend their lives in darkness. They have a natural aversion to bright light.

If you've ever had the misfortune of living in a place infested by vermin, like roaches or mice, you've seen them scatter when you turn on a light. That's exactly what happens when you call on the powers of the Sun. All the spirits of darkness flee.

As soon as the light's gone though, you can bet they'll be back. That's why many Christian exorcisms fail. Christ is a solar deity in many ways. The Crucifixion is a good example of a Solar Initiation. It's the shaman's death and resurrection as a solar being. When the exorcist calls on Christ, he gets a blast of Solar power that will work to get the spirit off and out of the victim.

It just doesn't do anything to keep it gone if the core problems aren't addressed.

So use Solar power in a fight for immediate effect, and then go back to Mars and/or Saturn to keep it gone.

## The Assistant

As I mentioned above, the Crucifixion of Christ is the symbol of the Solar Initiation. Solar initiations are painful experiences. Mine was awful to go through, but worth every scorched minute of it. As it says of Christ, for the joy set before him, he endured the cross.

When you go through a true, deep solar initiation, you go through a truly painful time. The rituals designed to bring you into contact with your Holy Guardian Angel, your Supernatural Assistant, or even your Genius Spirit are solar initiations. The Abramelin rite and Liber Samekh are good examples of the kind of deep initiation that brings a painful transformation of the magician. The Supernatural Assistant of the Greek Magical Papyri, in my opinion, is the prototype of the entity that became over time the "Holy Guardian Angel."

It's an entity that protects you from the worst case scenarios in life. It also serves as an intermediary spirit between you and other spirits. It's an essential companion, in my opinion, for performing Goetic works. In various African Traditional Religions, the sorcerer receives a particular spirit assistant, a type of familiar or fetch spirit who works with them for the rest of their magical careers in a very similar way.

The way I teach people to get in touch with this spirit is through a series of conjurations of Michael the Archangel of the Sun, the Genius Spirit, and then the Supernatural Assistant. Michael provides a gentle initiation, in theory, and lays out the foundation for the initiation to come. The Genius Spirit is an entity whose name is derived from your natal chart. This entity oversees your Fate, and I've found that working with this entity to contact your personal Solar Supernatural Assistant works.

The Genius is similar to the Assistant in some ways, but different in its role in your life. Everyone who was born has a Genius Spirit. This spirit works with the person throughout their lives whether they contact and commune with it or not.

# The Sun

The Supernatural Assistant is only given to Magicians. Its role is to be your personal bodyguard, to teach you how to be a Magician-King, and to act as a liaison to the various tribes of spirits we work with as magicians. I call on my Assistant every time I do magic. I speak its name aloud, and it appears before me.

I believe this is the same entity as the Holy Guardian Angel. People whose opinions I respect believe it's different. I'm a practical Taurus type person, and from what I've seen, the Supernatural Assistant I use and the Holy Guardian Angel those who have gone through the Abramelin rite work with are functionally the same.

There are a lot of silly myths about people's Holy Guardian Angel floating around. I met someone who believed they had sacrificed their HGA to Satan and that it was now scattered golden specks of angel dust in the aethers and that it needed to be reassembled and healed before they could contact and work with it. That ain't how it works, folks.

I suspect it's people like me trying to tell people who haven't gotten K&CHGA what it's like that breeds these kind of myths. It could also just be that the guy didn't know anything about what he was talking about, and just sort of made some shit up. I know spirits who answer to conjurations of Satan who would pretend to do just this kind of thing to get whatever they get out of fucking with people. Making someone think you've killed someone who could help them if they'd just ask is a good way to make sure they don't ask.

The Assistant will come to anyone who asks for it. It might take a while, and you may have to ask for a few months, but sincere asking is rewarded. "Ask, Seek, and Knock, and the Gates will be Opened unto You" is a good phrase to remember when it comes to the Solar Assistant.

Notice I call it a lot of things? That's because it does a lot of things. It's not my fault, and I'm sorry if it confuses you. It's a Supernatural assistant, it's like the Genius, it functions the same way as an HGA would, and it's a Solar Spirit. I think...

At the moment.

Okay, you're up to speed.

Now the Assistant is not something that you're going to get from this rite. I bring him up because he's important to you as a magician. Crowley once said something like "the primary aim of a magician should be the attainment of Knowledge and Conversation with the Holy Guardian Angel."

-51-

What is not common knowledge is that he wasn't really talking about the Holy Guardian Angel. He was talking about a state of being that can be reached by working with the Holy Guardian Angel. It's the result of a series of transformations that you can't really go through without an Assistant of the Solar Sphere. But Knowledge and Conversation with the Holy Guardian Angel is not the actual point; it's the key to the point. The state he wants you to get to is the self-aware augoeides state that can be reached via the conversations you have with the Holy Guardian Angel, that comes from the Knowledge you gain from the Work you do with the Holy Guardian Angel as you discover your true nature, remembering that you are a god in the flesh, and that you're here because you love how awesome this feels.

This is why K&CHGA should be one of the first real transformational magical acts a magician does. After that, you can do all things you set your mind to. Before that, you probably could anyway, but it would be harder and you'd spend a lot of time doing useless things that only almost get you what you want. Crowley's comment was true, but it should probably read something like, "The primary aim of an aspiring magician should be the attainment of Knowledge and Conversation with the Holy Guardian Angel so that his magical acts are empowered and effective." Through the Assistant, your rate of attainment can be greatly accelerated.

You really should do Abramelin, or Liber Samekh. You really should do the "Attaining a Supernatural Assistant" rite from the Greek Magical Papyri, or adapt the Stele of Jehu yourself to meet this spirit. It helps a lot.

The Solar rite that you'll be doing as part of this book will help form the foundation you'll need to eventually attain K&CHGA. You need a Solar framework, eyes that have been opened to see the Light of the Sun to be able to understand the things it says. The initiation prepares you, grants you the senses you'll need to have to be able to Commune with the entity.

# Venus

In the Neoplatonic cosmology, the Chain of Manifestation begins with an Idea in the Mind of God, and ultimately ends in the manifestation of the Idea here in the material realm, the world of the elements beneath the Sphere of the Moon. When the forces of the higher spheres pass from the Sphere of the Sun to the Sphere of Venus, the first forces that result in the physical manifestation of the original Idea are generated.

In the Golden Dawn, the Tree of Life shows a veil called "Paroketh" between Tiphareth, the Sphere of the sun, and the three spheres below, Netzach (the Sphere of Venus), Hod (the Sphere of Mercury), and Yesod (the Sphere of the Moon). These lower spheres are denser than those above, and Paroketh represents the curtain that separated the Holy of Holies from the rest of the world in the Temple of Solomon.

When a thing manifests, it grows denser as it descends through the spheres. In Saturn, an Idea is given its set Fate, its boundaries. In Jupiter, the essence of the Idea is expanded until it fills the boundaries set in Saturn. In Mars, the Idea is refined, disciplined, and given the force it needs to carve out and maintain its place in the world. In the Sun, it is further defined, given the power it needs to accomplish all the things it is destined to do as it manifests in the material realm. Then, it passes through Paroketh, and it begins to receive the forces that will coalesce and give a thing form and shape here Below.

The next three Spheres address things as they materialize in your Kingdom. Venus is the sphere of birth, where the Ideas above begin to manifest, among other things. Mercury is the sphere of measurement and exchange, and the Moon is the sphere of imagery, the final shape of things as they appear in the material realms.

Venus is the first stop as the Idea begins to manifest. It is the place where the Idea is actually *created* in our kingdoms on Earth where we can experience or express it. Venus is like a nebula in space, the birthplace of stars. Here the forces combine and interact. When a thing passes through Venus, it is beginning to manifest.

To put it into the most practical of terms I can think of, if your Kingdom were a business that sold physical products, like cell phones, Venus would best be represented as Production. In this department, raw materials are assembled and take shape. It is the birthing center of your products. It is the processes that are required to make the product. It is the assembly of the parts into the final product. Here the cell phone electronics are combined and sealed into their plastic cases.

But that's just a practical assessment. While the metaphor is apt, it completely robs Venus of her beauty, her depth, her passion for the pleasure of creation.

## The Core of Venus Magic

Ah, sweet Venus. She's the sphere of Creation. And procreation too! All things that manifest must pass through this sphere, and this is where the creative forces that will bring a thing into being come together. This is the sphere of the seed planted in soil, of spermatozoa uniting with egg, where pollen and stamen begin the process of creating fruit.

It is the sphere the Golden Dawn called the realm of "Natural Magic." I thought forests and trees and beasts and bunnies when I read that description, but I should probably have been thinking more about the birds and the bees than anything else. This sphere, as I found in my initiation into it, is *in fact,* the sphere of fucking in all its glorious splendor.

It is not the sphere of gratuitous sex, though. I mean, that can happen as a result of working in this sphere, but if you lose sight of the production aspect that is at the core while you're working this sphere (represented best by, you know, copulation, pregnancy, and birth), you may very easily find yourself in an uncomfortable situation.

All Venus rites produce a "child" of some kind. Remember that. And children, as parents well know, are the embodiment of responsibility. They bring pleasures and pains unimaginable to the non-parent mind. In magic, our children may not be human genetic experiments, but they are still present, and every bit as complicated as raising a human child.

Long after you think you'll be dealing with issues related to the magic you do in Venus, it will still pop up and ask for cash, or need to be bailed out of jail in the wee hours of the morning, or it may be asking you to babysit your grandkids. It's not always bad, but I've found every rite we do creates something that has unanticipated lasting impacts on our lives.

When you are bringing things into manifestation within your Kingdom, be aware that you are going to have to live with what you've created, regardless of whether you are prepared to deal with it or not. There will always be consequences in your material realm when you do Venus magic, whether it is for opulent luxury, creative inspiration, or a love spell to bring you the person of your dreams.

## The Faces of Venus Magic

Although the core of Venus magic is the act of creation, there's a lot that goes into getting you to the moment of creation. In procreative terms, the meeting, the establishment of a relationship, and the physical consummation are all parts of that process. In manufacturing terms, the inspiration, the resource gathering, and the production of the product are all parts of the process. Venus rules over the whole thing. She's up there on her clam shell throne looking down on it all.

### *Relationships*

Venus gathers people together around a common cause. Any group that's gathered around a cause has done so by the powers of Venus. Any time people interact, they are relating to one another, or they're in a *relationship*. This applies as much to business partnerships and alliances of nations as it does to matters of love and romance. All relationships, all interactions between people gathered around any common cause, whether it's the Tea Party conservatives or the Wall Street Occupiers, they are all ruled by Venus.

Some relationships are more special to us than others. Family relationships are beyond our control, but the "family" is the core idea or common cause that unites the individual parents, siblings, and cousins of any family. Bad blood within families can be resolved using the powers of the sphere of Venus. Likewise, family get-togethers can be blessed to bring happiness when they're planned. People in your family can be influenced towards your own specific causes through her sphere as well.

Spousal relationships are pretty special too. Any partnership between two people based on love and/or sex is under her auspices. If you're single and looking for love, she's the one to call. If you're in a spousal relationship and you need some help working through issues, she's the one to call. Venus knows how to soothe tempers and bring couples back together who are united in love. Don't be afraid to call on her.

It applies to all types of relationships. Your friends are drawn together for a common cause: to have fun and enjoy life together. Business networks are drawn together for the common cause of getting ahead, making more money, expanding your budget so you can live more like a King in your kingdom. Any group of people you interact with has been drawn together within the boundaries of your Kingdom through the powers of Venus. It's a process, and most of us participate in the process pretty passively.[5]

In your Kingdom, you don't have to be passive. Taking authority in your Kingdom requires taking authority over your relationships. I don't mean turn into a raging dickhead, either. Nor do I mean that you become a manipulative person, even though that's a constant temptation. I'm talking about taking an active role in making your relationships in your life work together to bring you closer to your overall Kingdom goals.

You do this by setting the common cause that's at the core of the relationship. You determine what cause you want the people in your life to be gathered around, and the specific goals you gather them together to accomplish. For friends, I like to keep it at enjoyment of life and mutual support. That's a great cause. But be ready to contribute to the things you do with your friends. Set up something that will be fun. Set aside time and space, make arrangements, and have a good time. Take an active role.

Set up a business group of your peers that meets to discuss tips and tricks of the trade. I hang out with bloggers and occult authors, and we exchange ideas. In my fundamentalist Christian days, I went to a men's prayer group in the mornings at 6:00 a.m. to pray and talk with other men. We happened to be all white collar workers, and it was sort of like a fraternal Order in practice, exchanging insider trading information, letting people know about opportunities, hooking one another up with clients when we could.

Set something up for yourself along your own interests. Be the catalyst among a peer group. Announce an idea, a cause, and see who Venus brings together to participate.

---

5  I hate alliteration, really I do.

When I started doing magic for real, I found a lot of power in it. I was amazed and wanted to talk to other magicians who were doing magic and finding power in it, and so I hit the occult message boards. The problem was that there weren't many people doing magic that I could talk to about it. That is, there weren't many people doing it the way I did it, with Trithemius, archangels, my HGA, and at the time, demons of the Lemegeton's Goetia.

So I started my blog to get some information out there about what I do and how powerful it is. I wanted to be able to talk to people who had been through what I was going through, but no one I could find was willing to discuss it. Over the years, I've written about what I do, taught some people some stuff, and developed a pretty advanced group of magician colleagues I can do some pretty neat things to the world with.

All this is under the power of Venus. You Work with her to set up relationships that will bring you the things you need in your kingdom. And when you start looking at the kinds of things you want in your life, the kinds of common goals you'll establish, you'll quickly find that most of the things you want involve something pleasurable to you.

## *Pleasures*

Venus is the realm of pleasures too, but I hesitate to touch on that. People rarely need to be encouraged to seek their pleasures. Magicians face a special kind of temptation when it comes to the pleasures of Venus. There's nothing that feels better than creating the world through magical practice. It can get to be addictive. There's a constant temptation to just do magic for magic's sake.

And honestly, I tend to encourage that kind of thing. It's awesome, and you learn a lot from experimentation. If a thing can be done magically or mundanely, I usually pick magically because I like to do things that way.

The danger in this is that if you're doing magic that you don't really need to do, you're eventually going to call up something that you haven't really prepared for. In the period of a single month, I had three people who needed help getting things straightened out in their spheres because they just did magic for magic's sake, without realizing the consequences. Unintended consequences will bite you in the ass. It happens, it's usually okay, and it's not something that should keep you from doing magic, but you should never lose sight of the fact that every magical act is going to have a consequence.

The pleasures of Venus are always part of the manifestation, production, or creation process. Orgasm is the enticement to procreate, perpetuating the species. The pleasurable effects of drugs are the enticement to learn from our herbal brothers and sisters about the nature of the Spiritus Mundi.

Pleasures of all types can provide gates to other realms, or grant abilities necessary to get through particular situations in life. But these pleasures go along with the creative process, and people who are only in it for the pleasures of creation, and not what they are creating, can quickly manifest sexual disorders or get lost in drug addiction.

In fact, this is one of the weapons of Venus, the ability to drive both humans and otherworldly creatures mad with desires, to bind them in chains of their lust. It's even mentioned in the Orphic hymn.

And there are other dark aspects of Venus to watch out for. She is the primal woman, who, when scorned, hath fury unmatched in any hell. She is perfect to call on in matters of avenging abuse in relationships; she will not stand idly by as someone brings harm in the guise of love. She is dark and terrible and fearsome indeed.

You should be really careful.

That said, Venus is fucking brilliant! The powers there feel like orgasm, or a really pleasant high, a friendly warm buzz, a glow of laughter and friendship as well as a latent heat of physical passion soon to be released. It's awesome to work in this sphere.

## Production

As I stated in the beginning of this section, the most practical and pragmatic description of the powers of the Sphere of Venus would be the Production department of a major company. We're talking raw industrial steaming production. Here the metals that have been purified are melted and combined into alloys that are then shaped into material things. Here the products are pumped out and over to distribution. Here is the sphere where supply shortages, industrial sabotage, or equipment breakdown impacts are to be found. This is your sphere of production above all else.

Think about what it is that your Kingdom produces. My Kingdom produces occult instruction manuals and entertainment. I'm also responsible for producing all the things that generate an income in my life. But there are other aspects to this too. I produce service products in my office. I produce craft products with my kids. I produce intangible products in my family, in terms of memories, experiences, education, and guidance. Every action I take has an impact on the world, and creates something as a result. At the most minute level, the power of Venus is manifesting in my life at every moment.

Production issues are generally signs of a disturbance or blockage in the flow of the forces of Venus into your life. Writer's block is a serious example of this malaise. The treatment is the conjuration of the Intelligence of the Sphere, questions to discern the cause and a probable solution, and then taking action to implement the advice received.

## *Opulence*

The last aspect of Venus I'd like to discuss is the opulence factor. As a Taurus, I can tell you all about the joys and pleasures that luxury provides. Having high-quality, well-made things is a pleasure to the senses. It feels good. And in this world, there are plenty of things that feel bad. Having a nice, opulent, luxurious part of your life to go to and just feel pleasure in is a kind of therapy.

Not only that, but luxury is also a sound value. I've bought cheap shoes, and I've bought custom shoes, and custom shoes generally last longer. The same is true of couches, carpets, dishware, and vehicles. Luxurious items don't just look better than common things; they last longer and retain their value better over time. It's better business sense to save up for the more expensive, well-made items than it is to make do with something that costs less and breaks sooner.

As you tap into the sphere of Venus in your Kingship, don't be afraid to channel some of that into making your life a bit luxurious. Don't feel guilty, it's okay to enjoy the fruits of your labor. Venus produces fruits, and then you're supposed to enjoy them.

Jupiter is the force of expansion, but Venus is the sphere in which this expansion takes shape here in the physical realm below. This is where the gold increases, the luxuriant lifestyle appears. This is where the attendants and servants see to our needs. This is where the décor of the kingdom appears, in fine quality and expensive tastes.

There's a severe mindset many of us have that robs us of the enjoyment of luxurious items. When we are productive-type people who like to get things done, we can get all wrapped up in the production and forget to enjoy ourselves. Working in Venus teaches you that enjoying the benefits of our work is okay.

The pleasures arise from the creative process, production occurs when the prepared ingredients are brought together, and the opulence comes from the movement of products into the world at large. Venus is a sphere of much power, joy, and success.

# Mercury

As discussed in the description of Venus, the Sphere of Mercury is situated within the zone of spheres below the Sun, which the Golden Dawn puts below Paroketh, the veil separating the manifest world from the Holy of Holies in the Temple of Solomon. The lower three spheres, Venus, Mercury, and the Moon, are the most material of the celestial spheres, and in these spheres an Idea on its way towards manifestation here in the material realm picks up the last little bits of the framework of forces that it needs to come into existence, the momentum of its existence, and its final shape.

## The Flow

The sphere of Mercury is always in motion. That is perhaps the most important thing to understand about this sphere, that at its essence, Mercury *flows*. It moves. At room temperature, the metal Mercury is a liquid and cannot be grasped. It can only be contained in glass or iron because it amalgamates to almost everything else. It is highly adaptive and forms bonds to almost everything it touches.

It is this nature of pervasiveness, connectivity, and *flow* that is expressed in all the things Mercury rules. Communication is the flow of information, and its exchange. Technology is the practical application of the flow of information and observation. Writing is the ability to shape information into a symbol that can then be passed to others to enable this flow of information.

When you think about Mercury as being at its essence "flow," it makes sense that Mercury would also rule the realm of business transactions. Business is the flow of products and services from those who have them to those who need them. Money is exchanged, and most business processes are related to tracking the exchange and flow of money, goods, and services.

Business is the art and science of understanding where the money comes from, where it goes, and at what rate and frequency.

Mercury rites for businesses will address the flow of money, goods, and services in some way every time. If you require a lot of traffic to make a profit, it will increase the flow of traffic to your web site, or to your physical store. If you need to make a specific connection to people who need what you offer, Mercury will direct the flow of information about your services to the target audience. It aids in Marketing, the communication of your offered goods and services to those who need and can afford to buy them.

## Classification, Correspondence, and Research

Mercury is also the sphere that rules the classification and correspondence. Information is classified and sorted into systems and symbols that can be used to understand and interact with the world. This allows discernment, the ability to observe and gather information, analyze it and group it in different categories that relate to one another, and reach a conclusion about what needs to be done to accomplish your desired outcome.

In our magical activities, we rely a great deal on the correspondences between things material and things celestial to create and influence the manifestation of our world. This classification of the properties of various things that end up in the tables of correspondence in Agrippa, or in 777, also falls under the sphere of Mercury. By understanding the different things that correspond to a spirit, we can create a talisman that they can work with more readily to accomplish the changes in our world that we desire.

Medical diagnosis is the act of observing symptoms and deducing the cause so that a treatment can be implemented. Education is the process of learning the classification systems and filling this framework with data that can be understood by its position in the classification system relative to everything else.

The Periodic Table of Elements is a good example of this. You learn something about the elements just by where they are located on the Table. You see what their density is by relating each to the ones around it. The Table of Elements shows how things we touch and feel are the logical progressive accumulation of atomic particles that interact in unique ways as they are combined in different ways.

# Mercury

Mercury is the force that enables problem solving. When faced with a problem, you observe, analyze, and make connections between different aspects of the problem and other things until you come up with a solution.[6]

Where Venus is your production line, Mercury is the research branch of your company. You gather data, see how it is related, and how it can be mingled and combined to create a new product. The schematics, the symbols that teach how to put it all together, are designed and sent over to the production department (over in Venus) where the product is actually created. Research and Development is the cooperation of Mercury and Venus.

## Thought and Memory

Mercury is also the realm of thought and memory. Thoughts are always flowing through your mind. It almost never stops processing, putting things together that it sees, coming up with new conglomerations of data or things. Meditation reveals this most clearly. If you've ever tried to sit and not think, you know how hard it is to do. Your mind never stops. The very best meditational techniques work with this fact instead of against it, being based on the understanding that the mind is supposed to flow, and using that to your advantage. Instead of trying to suppress all thoughts, you observe them and use the diagnostic utility of your mind to identify where the thoughts arise from and where they go to when you move on. This observation and classification is still Mercurial, thinking, thoughtful, contemplative, but it is used to bring understanding of your Self in its purest form.

The sphere of Mercury is also known for being capricious and witty. The trickster deities of different pantheons often express Mercurial qualities. A quickness of mind, the ability to quickly make unexpected connections between words and symbols and ideas that others do not make is the epitome of wit.

I'd like to point out something rather obvious that Mercury also rules. The techniques in this series are all based on Hermetic principles and philosophies. Hermes is the god of Mercury. All the magic you've done in this series has been Hermetic magic. Mercury is the sphere of Hermetic Magic, and again, it is all about the management of the flow of power through you and into the world around you.

---

6 Note that the Latin root of the word "solution" is "solve," as in "Solve et Coagula," or dissolve and reform. You dissolve a problem into its component parts and put the parts back together in a way that you prefer to come up with a "solution."

By passing through these spheres, you are moving through the heavens. You are communicating with the Intelligences of the Spheres. You are consciously tracking the flow of Ideas as they descend through the heavens and manifest here in the material realm. You are drawing down the authority to rule your Kingdom as King.

## Mercury's Influence in your Kingdom

In your Kingdom, the rules you create to govern are expressed, communicated using the network of Mercurial forces. As King, you need to know the communication lines well to use them most effectively. By harmonizing the forces of Mercury, you will be able to get your rulership out into the manifest realm. Clear communication of intent, of governmental edicts, of rules and consequences are essential to running a Kingdom.

Mercury also rules the education level of your Kingdom. How much do you know as a King? If you haven't been exposed to many different things, your mind won't be able to make new and innovative connections to bring your Kingdom increased wealth and power. A small stream can only accommodate small boats. Small boats can't carry much stuff. The wider and deeper your knowledge base, the more you can accomplish.

The attainment of skills and understanding are under the auspices of Mercury. Whether you focus this on gaining a wide variety of skills or specializing in one particular area of expertise is up to you. When you've obtained the skills, market them, and ask Mercury to improve the communication between you and your clients/customers in the language of commerce.

By entering the Gate of Mercury, you're able to see the flow of different aspects of your life within your Kingdom. The paths of emotional responses and reflexive acts can be mapped out and adjusted. Destructive behaviors can be identified and altered. Stagnant areas in your life can be identified, and with the powers of this sphere, you can bring life-giving *flow* to these areas. Mercury is the sphere of analysis and categorization. It puts data sets together in ways that can be used and manipulated. It presents information in a way that lets you extract the bits and pieces you need that are related.

If you're called to be a healer, the specific powers you direct to accomplish specific results can be identified, developed, and increased within this sphere. You can learn to mingle them in ways that are most effective to treat the ailments you address. You can develop the skill to see where a patient's flow of health has been blocked, what has blocked the flow, and how to unblock it.

And of course the business of your Kingdom must be addressed from the sphere of Mercury. Profitable transactions are the exchange of currency for goods and services. This exchange is a type of communication, with you speaking in goods and services, and your employers or clients/customer base speaking in currency. "Money talks," as they say.

The more varied your services (job skills for your work for example) or products are, the more people you will be able to sell to. Having wide varieties of skills and products is a Mercurial trait. The Jack of All Trades, Master of None is a good example of a Mercurial archetype. You have to be careful, because in Mercury, it's easy to spread yourself too thin. Let yourself pick up a nice mixture of harmonious skills or products, and you'll find Mercury will work well within your sphere to produce the profits you seek.

On the other end of the spectrum, but still within the realm of Mercury's influence, is the specialist. The better you are at performing the skills you have acquired, or the higher the quality of your products, the more you'll be able to charge for either. The intellectual specialist is also an archetype of Mercury. Scientists, doctors, and physicists are examples of these types.

And remember the essence of Mercury is *flow*. The business of your Kingdom needs to flow. In my side business online, I need a steady flow of traffic to my web site to get new business. I also need a steady flow of products to maintain repeat business. Flow is the key to commerce.

# The Moon

As discussed previously, the Sphere of the Moon lies within the zone of spheres below the Sun. The Moon holds a special place in the Chain of Manifestation. Being the last sphere before manifestation, all things must pass through the Moon. Not only that, but because she moves around the Earth every day, she goes through an astrological conjunction with all the other planets and fixed stars. She is absorbing and reflecting the forces of the other spheres every day. She's like a cup that goes to each planetary wellspring, and then pours out her contents upon the manifest world.

Or in other words, the Moon is sort of like a Wandering Womb, receiving the seed from all the other planets and then birthing the outcome into the manifest world. She is the intermediary to the rest of the spheres. She is the most important of all the spheres when we're either heading up through the heavens on a journey of Contemplation, or bringing the powers down to the Earth to manifest desired outcomes. The Moon is the Gate between the Macrocosm and the Microcosm. Getting in good with this sphere will expand your magical powers greatly.

## The Moon and the Shape of Things

Specifically, the sphere of the Moon provides the outermost shape of an idea as it passes into materialization. In the plant kingdom, the Moon rules over the leaves, the outermost extremities of the plant. Different planets rule the stems, the roots, and the bark, but the leaves are under the Moon.

This is why the Moon is the realm of Illusions. People see the outermost image of a thing and believe they are seeing the thing itself. The truth known to Hermetic practitioners aware of the chain of manifestation is that all things are manifestations of much more complex and intricately woven forces from each of the seven planetary spheres. We know there's more than meets the eye when we look at things.

However, we also know that all seven spheres were concentrated into the final sphere of the Moon prior to manifesting. As a result, the trained eye can see aspects of each of the planets in proportion in the final form. The trick is learning to translate what we see into the seven parts that have combined to form the final shape. Most of us don't start out with that level of discernment, so we must be careful not to judge a book by its cover, as the saying goes.

## Materialization

The Moon waxes and wanes, grows and shrinks. Her sphere rules over the waxing and waning of all things in existence. Things don't generally just appear overnight. Situations in our kingdoms that require our attention build up slowly over time, and the sooner we become aware of a forming problem in our kingdom, the sooner we can address it.

Things we want in our life take a while to manifest too. Suppose you wanted to buy a diamond ring for your partner. You'd save up the money, go shopping, pick out the one you want, purchase it, and then present it to them. It's an incremental process of gathering information, specific details, and the resources to manifest the desire. The results of our magic manifest the same way, gradually, building up over time.

The Moon also wanes, decreasing. She rules over the fading away of things and situations in our life as well. Again, it's a process that doesn't take place all at once. The outer form of a material object erodes, oxidizes, or gets worn down over time, losing its mint-fresh newness, and gaining in character. Even when things disappear from our lives in an instant, like in a car crash, there is still a series of events leading up to the diminishment of the material object. When a tumor is removed, there is a period of recovery before full health returns. The negative impact of the tumor gradually fades from the patient's life.

So the forces of the Moon rule the waxing and waning, a gradual manifestation and a gradual return to the un-manifest that all things in the material realm go through. Passing through the Gate of the Moon puts you in harmony with this process of waxing and waning. At this moment in your life, there are things that are coming into being, and things that are passing away. Passing through the Gate of the Moon makes you more aware of these things, and increases your ability to see the things changing from manifest to un-manifest.

Now I mentioned illusion above, and that's another major part of the Sphere of the Moon. Because this is the sphere in the chain of manifestation that gives a thing its final form, we can see the forms of things here that have not yet, or for some reason cannot yet, materialize in the physical realm. Dreams and visions are images, shapes, forms that appear in your mind's eye that are not necessarily physical, but take on a form that you can see. In this aspect, passing through the Gate of the Moon can improve your spiritual vision, enabling you to see spirits and interpret visions more accurately.

## The Moon's Forces in your Kingdom

In this rite, we are specifically addressing passing through the Gate of the Moon to receive initiation and insight into the ways the Lunar influence affects our Kingdom. The current that we tap into in Jupiter has passed through all the other spheres on the way here, and in the Moon it receives its final shape, the way it will appear here below, in the material realm.

Passing through the Gate of the Moon will help us rule our Kingdoms by granting us the vision to see the forces working to manifest things in our lives, to understand the process of manifestation and to time our manifestation rites appropriately, and the ability to see through illusions to the true nature of things below, while also granting the ability to hide the true nature of things when necessary.

### *Vision*

Many of my students have talked about how much trouble they have seeing spirits. Most of the magic I teach involves conjuring spirits, so not being able to see them can be problematic, especially for beginners who aren't entirely convinced that what they are doing is working. My assurances that they don't have to sense the spirit for it to be effective work to assuage their doubts until they have proven it to themselves in most cases, but it's still frustrating.

Everyone has different levels of natural ability to see the spiritual realm. Some of us block that off as we grow older, while others simply can't see anything. All things we experience in our kingdoms pass through this Gate before manifesting here below, and as a result, it is the sphere of the Moon that we can turn to in order to gain insight into the occult, hidden nature of things we are experiencing.

On the flip side, it is also the sphere of the Moon that allows us to hide things from the sight of others. As a practicing occultist, there are times when I need to cover my tracks, and leave no trace in the aethyrs of what I've done, or who it was that did it. Invisibility from detection is also a power of the moon.

This is also the realm of glamours. There are times when it behooves us to appear differently than we really are, to accentuate certain features over others. Interviews come to mind, where we need to appear to be exactly the right fit for the position we're applying for. When we've passed through the Lunar Gate, we can offer a quick word to Gabriel as we head into the meeting to present ourselves in a way that shows the value of adding us to the team.

## *Materialization*

The Moon is the sphere that rules over the way a thing takes shape in the world. This includes the progression of its lifespan within existence. As the Moon increases, so also do things come into being, a little at a time, a consistent predictable pattern of accretion until it is whole. Passing through this Gate brings insight into the manifestation process itself, the waxing of relationships, situations, plans, plots, as well as material things we are crafting and building in our Kingdoms.

As things come into being, so they also pass away. As soon as a thing has materialized in this realm in its final form, it begins to fade away, returning piece by piece to the spheres it came from. Whether it's a new car that starts getting scratched and dented as you drive it through the world, or a relationship with a team of co-workers on a project, all things that come into being in this realm pass away.

As we gain insight and understanding of this sphere and its role in our Kingdoms, we learn to plan our rites in the timing of the Moon. In general, we try to plan our rites of manifestation during times of the waxing moon, bringing things down into the material realm as the light that the Moon reflects grows. When we want to make things go away, we time our rites to coincide with the waning of the Moon.

It's funny: there are a lot more rites to make things come into being than there are to make things go away. It's no dark mystery that things pass from the world of the seen to the world of the unseen, but we seem to be focused mostly on manifestation of things in our lives. Learning to understand the power of the Waning Moon is important. Half the time we're alive, the Moon is going to be ready to help make things go away.

I do a lot of wealth magic, or at least I used to. I got pretty good at it. Making money is remarkably easy once you get the hang of it. You do a rite, you follow up on the inspiration, and you sell the result. The hardest part is following up on a project that comes from Above to make you money, in my experience.

But I never really got into the waning side of things. Gaining wealth is also decreasing poverty. Income is increased by the decrease of out-go. Decrease your debt, and you've increased your net value. Removing bad situations at your employment can be more effective than trying to create a better situation in another job. Reducing risk increases your chances of success.

Knowing that the manifestation cycle of all things in existence is ruled by the Moon does not limit us in our magical approach; it simply guides us to taking a more effective course that is in harmony with the prevailing forces of the moment.

## *Follow the Light*

In the previous section I talked about timing your rites to coincide with the Moon, materializing during waxing phases, dematerializing during waning phases, and that's important and good, solid, practical advice for ruling your Kingdom. But there's something else to consider about the Moon and where the Light goes when she's waxing and waning that can give us insight in our own personal growth as magicians.

The light of the Moon is a reflection of the light of the Sun. While it appears to grow and shrink to us here below, it's an illusion. The same amount of the Moon is always in the Light of the Sun, except when the Earth passes between the two during a lunar eclipse. The light is always there, and the moon is always "full"; it just happens to be pointing somewhere else when she's not Full.

When she's Full, all the Light of the Sun, a sphere above the Moon, is being reflected down to us here Below. The powers of the higher spheres are being focused in a downward direction towards the material realm. As she's increasing, it's a good time to do materialization magic, obviously. Farmers plant their seeds during waxing moon phases to get a bigger harvest.

But when she's waning, it's a good time to plant your seeds Above. You follow the Light. As the Moon turns her face upwards to the heavens above, the spheres beyond the Moon, we should also be tuning our spiritual magic, our Theurgical rites towards the heavens above. The power and wisdom to rule our Kingdoms well comes from Above, from our brothers and sisters, from our Source in the eternal divine. Waning moon phases are a good time to travel the aethyrs and recharge, receive new initiations, deeper understanding, and more power to apply here below.

# The Sphere of Saturn

When we pass through the Gate of Saturn, we receive an initiation into the first planetary sphere an Idea passes into as it leaves the infinite light of the Mind of God. It is the realm in which the beginning and the end are determined for a thing's manifestation. Every physical object or social situation, every thought or impulse we receive, manifest, and experience here in the world of our physical senses has a beginning and an ending point. The point at which it first manifests in space and time is assigned in the sphere of Saturn, as is the exact moment that it will leave the manifest realm and return to its Source, shedding layers of manifestation as it ascends.

Saturn is thus the realm of boundaries. Borders. It limits the unlimited, it binds things to their destiny. It is this binding quality that makes it so useful in dealing with Underworld entities who don't have the comfort and happiness of mankind at heart. By working with the spirits of this sphere, you can learn to identify and set boundaries of things you create, and to manipulate the boundaries of things that already exist that are not to your liking.

Note that by changing the boundaries of things in the Sphere of Saturn, you are moving things at the most fundamental level. You're changing fate when you play in Saturn.

I've had some proponents of free will argue that if you can change fate, it is by nature no longer "fate." My current understanding based on my experiences in this sphere is that if a fate is changed, it is changed by the direct interference of beings who exist below the level of Saturn in the chain of manifestation. In other words, the change in fate was itself fated. Everything that will happen has already been decreed, but while we are viewing the unfolding of creation in ignorance of future events, it will always seem to be the result of free will and unpredictable interactions of infinite variables.

Anyway, it sure seems like you can change fate by working in Saturn, even if you're fulfilling your fate in the process. Doesn't really matter much to me, as long as I get what I want or a good reason for not wanting it anymore.

Since you receive your end point in Saturn, he's become associated with Death. Death comes for us all, King or pauper, and in Death we are all equal. A common image of Saturn is Death himself, carrying his scythe. That's one of the reasons I refer to the Sphere of Saturn as Mr. Grim. In my writing. Not in person. Not to his face. Er, facelessness. Just doesn't seem like a very good idea at the time.

In general, Saturn's influence is usually pretty negative. He's the Greater Malefic, after all. Disease, famine, and death are his calling cards. But he's not all bad.

Once you've accepted that you have a beginning and an end within the confines of your existence, you know, your "life," Saturn's not that terrible of a place to visit. I'm more at home there these days than I was before I hit thirty, that's for sure.

Along the path of my initiations, I received various Visions of the Spheres, and they prepared me to understand and process the whole "circle of life" thing. When I finally integrated the forces of the Solar initiation, one of the first things I did was go visit Saturn, and there I fell in love.

Previous Saturn rites had left me depressed, but this time it was so different. Instead of feeling depressed, I found myself encouraged by the boundaries I faced in life, and aware that they are not set firmly in place, but serve as placeholders to support the unfolding of my life. Like pylons on a bridge, the energies of Saturn serve to support the weight of our endeavors.

The power of Saturn in the magician's sphere manifests as the power to set, or reset, the boundaries of our empire. Knowing yourself leads to knowing your limitations, but knowing Saturn leads to knowing how to move your limitations out a bit at a time. Bigger vaults means more room for the energies of Jupiter to fill with the treasures you seek in money rituals. Raising your expectations provides more room for opportunities. Raising your standards results in higher quality of character. Moving the boundaries of your mind releases you from the prison of your fear. Tearing down the walls of your heart makes room for love to flow into and out of your experience.

The power of Saturn is infinite because it is the power of making things finite. Looking back now, I see that the depression I felt came from the powerlessness I felt when I surveyed the boundaries of my life. These boundaries are firmly ensconced only by my attachment to them.

Barriers, walls, limitations—these things can seem to be negative, if your desires are beyond their limits. But at the same time, the walls support the roof, the dam stores the water, and the bones provide the support that lets us live as more than amorphous blobs. The skin limits us, keeps us from spilling out in a pile of goo, protects us from the intrusions of the malefic forces of nature.

Yet Saturn is cast as a malefic. Its role of death and binding are detrimental when passive. If we don't expand the boundaries, we outgrow them, and feel like we're wearing a suit two sizes too small. But when activated through magic, when approached through the heightened awareness of the magician who has integrated the forces of the other planetary spheres, Saturn is a beautiful friend, full of love in his own grim way, a helper and a guide, a focuser of the forces that follow in his footsteps.

He's also a lot like the Godfather. You want shit done, and you have a good relationship with him, he gets shit done. Just treat him with respect.

## Defining your Kingdom

How far can you go in life? Right now, as you are today. How far can you go in your career path with your experience and training and credentials, for example? I'm at the end of my career path with my current boundaries. I can't get to the next level without getting a certification or a college degree. I work government contracts by day to support my nightly pursuits of the dark arts. Federal law requires a degree or certification, or both for the next level of my field. I have to get that before I can go further here. I've reached the limit.

As a father, I'm in a stage of parenting that I will be in for another three years. My youngest kids are both in elementary school, and in three years the youngest will be going into middle school. The kid stage of my fatherhood will be over, and the pre-teen age will have begun. I haven't hit that limit yet; that boundary still lies ahead.

Where are your boundaries at right now in different areas of your life? What are the roles you find yourself in? This is, or at least has been, your fate. This is what you were meant to do so far. Have you checked out your life lately?

Get to know your boundaries. I like to make bulleted lists with outline levels. I can't help it; I'm a Technical Writer. The main bullet is the area of life, and sub bullets are aspects. I write up a list, and then think about each area, think about where I'm at and what I'm doing in that role in life. I think about where I see myself in the future in these different areas. I note to myself where the limits are, and think about whether or not I like those particular limitations.

You know my career, and how I've reached the upper limit? All I have to do is get the degree or certification, and that will expand my limitations to a few more rungs up the corporate ladder. I could make it to Vice President or some executive management level in five years or so, if I did that.

You'll note I'm not doing that any time soon. I'm not taking it off the table entirely as an option, but one thing I've learned about a Saturnian limitation is that the end platform where one thing gets off and out of your life can be a platform to a whole new area. You don't have to expand your limitations in an area of your life that you want to get rid of. You can just close out the current processes in that aspect of your life as you complete the required tasks, and then move on to something else.

You can end the things you don't like, at any time. The longer you take to make sure you've fulfilled all your responsibilities in that part of your life, the less it will hurt to walk away from, but remember there is never anything in your life that you can't walk away from if you're willing to accept the consequences. When addressing a sticky situation in your life, start with the knowledge, the truth that you could find a way to leave the situation. Everything else seems to fall into perspective for me when I begin with the knowledge that everything ends.

## Working with Saturn

Did I mention I went to Saturn after going through the Sun? That is, after attaining Knowledge and Conversation with my Holy Guardian Angel? After I'd done some magic for a while, and gone through the steps of being initiated by the Intelligences of the spheres all leading up to the Sphere of Saturn?

Just checking to make sure I mentioned all that. I didn't go to Saturn first. Don't go to Saturn first.

I don't want to hear, "I didn't think you meant it," or "I couldn't help it, I'm a DAREDEVIL, just like my old man" in an email. I will charge you a *lot* of money if you go to Saturn first, get some kind of *death curse*, and then come crawling to me to fix it when I warned you fair and square right up front. Don't go to Saturn first. There's a *reason* it's across the Abyss in that Golden Dawn/Thelemite cosmology thing.

Did I scare you enough?

Good.

Now, relax, you wouldn't really get a death curse. That's just bullshit to make a point. You're going to the realm of Death; take it seriously. It feels like dying when you go through a Solar Initiation, but when you go into the Sphere of Saturn, you realize what a drama queen you were being when you thought that back in the warm lands of the Sun. Real death is sobering. This is a realm you want to treat with respect. Mr. Grim is a formidable companion.

That doesn't mean you can't have fun with it if you have a morbid sense of humor. Just don't crack any jokes in his presence.

When you Work with Saturn's spirits, have a Solar talisman handy, at the least. It can get dark and cold fast, and having a heat and light source with you will come in handy.

When I first conjured Cassiel of Saturn, I felt a heavy and intense feeling fill the air. Subsequent visits have varied in intensity, but I seldom end a rite of Saturn without spending some time in meditation on another sphere related to my desired intent. Or I hang out with my Assistant in my astral temple discussing the things that went on Above. It gives me time to ground out the forces.

All the spirits of Saturn are dangerous and should be treated like loaded weapons. Keep them pointed away from yourself. Work with a circle between you and them, and a triangle too. You'll note that both are present on the Table of Practice I provide with this course. You'll also note that if you do the ritual properly, the spirits are inside a triangle inside a circle, and then there's you, outside, and you're within yet another circle on consecrated ground.

The rite is built in a way that keeps spirits you're not interested in that might be hanging around from getting into the crystal, and the Table is built in a way that keeps the spirit from reaching you too. Agrippa teaches that the circle is infinite to spirits, which is what keeps them out. They hit the geometry and just circle around. The table of Practice is sufficient.

## Saturn's Forces in your Kingdom

The forces of Saturn manifest in many ways in your kingdom both for your benefit and as challenges for you to overcome. Learning to identify the forces of Saturn as they manifest in your kingdom can also help you learn how to direct these forces as you see fit.

### *Binding*

> *"I will give you the keys of the kingdom of heaven; and whatever you bind on earth shall have been bound in heaven, and whatever you loose on earth shall have been loosed in heaven."*
>
> —Matthew 16:19

A binding ritual is the act of taking a person or spirit and placing a boundary around them that limits their ability to affect the world around them in ways you do not wish them to. It works on situations in your life, too. You can place limits on situations or people from the Sphere of Saturn. You do so by conjuring the spirit using the rite below, and when the spirit is present, instead of saying the Orphic Hymn (or after if you want to include it), you present your case.

When presenting your case to a spirit, don't assume he knows what's going on in your life, and all the details, and everything you mean when you say, "Bind the magicians working against me." Bind them in what way? From magic? They're magicians, called to pursue the dark arts the same as you. Will a spirit be able to override a calling by God? Maybe, if you do it right, but not very likely.

Be more specific to get better results. "Make strong all spiritual boundaries against any spirit or spell or scourge of man sent to bring any evil to me or my kingdom by the magic of Davey Jones" works much better. Don't be afraid to wax lyrical, either. The spirits like that flowery talk. They speak in holy languages, they speak in harmonies and song. They appreciate art, and artists. Use archaic language patterns if you are comfortable, or speak your oration in rhythm, beat, or rhyme. If you do it with respect and dignity, they will respond in the same manner.[7]

---

[7] Cheesy goth poetry is unacceptable, especially in Saturn. Dignity, man!

If you're not into that, speak clearly, in detail, and make clear points in your explanation. You want to mention at least the things that are going on in general that you are addressing. You want to mention specifically the parts of your life that you want to impact. You want to specify the people or situation you are targeting. You want to tell a story, basically. Provide the set and setting of what's going on, the characters and the interactions you want to affect, and then tell the spirit what you want it to do to make the changes you desire.

This is generally good advice for all conjure magic, but especially for Saturn. Mr. Grim knows the beginnings and endings of all things. He could look up what's going on at any moment in any situation, if he had to look things up, and tell you more about what's going on than anyone you could ever meet. He likes beginnings and endings. Explaining the situation and building the characters and the impacts and bringing it to an ending you desire seems to have a favorable effect with Mr. Grim.

But don't get too specific. Spirits work in their own ways, ways we cannot predict with 100% accuracy. I've had spirits manifest my exact stated results using methods that never occurred to me. Leave them some wiggle room to allow for factors you don't know about that could affect the outcome. For example, if someone is trying to steal your man, bind their efforts to steal your man, don't just have the spirit kill them. They may be serving some unknown purpose in the world, and while the spirit may be able to bind their specific machinations on your man, they may not be able to just kill them. So if you're over-specific, you get nothing. If you leave the spirit room to work their magic, within the boundaries of the situation you're addressing, you'll find your own magic gets more consistent results.

It's a balance that you pick up as you go along. Like most wisdom, it comes mostly from making mistakes. Don't be afraid to mess up. I've screwed things up pretty badly a couple times in my life learning magic, but the same forces that can run amok in your life can also fix it all up better than it was. You won't conjure up anything that someone can't put down, and the worst that could possibly happen is that something materializes you and eats you, dragging your soul into an eternity of suffering and pain.

And so far I haven't seen that happen, not even once. Wished it would happen to some people once or twice, but so far, nothing. And if those idiots can do magic and not get eaten, I guarantee you'll be fine. I mean, you've got to be smarter than most folks in this magical pursuit; you're reading my Work! Something's giving you really good taste in occult authors.[8]

## *Releasing*

Saturn magic is also good at releasing things. It's basically the same process as binding, but in reverse. The entities that place the boundaries are the best equipped to remove them.

Now, one of the first things Mr. Grim teaches you is that there is no such thing as "removing boundaries" in the sub-Saturnian realms. In other words, as long as a thing exists, it has limits. Saturn gives us access to the setters of limitation, and we are able to release the constraints holding us back, holding back situations, or blocking any of the spirits we might be working with. The constraints are released, and then settle back in somewhere else.

This is where being specific comes in handy again. If you want to move into the next career level, say you want the boundary of your career moved to the executive level, extending your reach so you can grasp the opportunity. If you want to break through a revenue ceiling, say so. If you want to move the boundaries of the pie slice representing your market share, say so. Show them the pie chart.

Leave some wiggle room, of course.

I've said, "Saturn use your powers to extend the boundaries of my Kingdom, granting me more resources and opportunities, and enabling me to reach my goals." It's generic as hell, and the results were just general in response. That's okay for expanding your kingdom. If you want to grow in your family, mention that. If you want more market share, mention that too. For Kingdom-expansion rites, I don't get too specific. I enjoy the adventure of exploring my expanded territories as they come.

## *Time*

Saturn is the sphere of time as well. I've gone on meditative journeys through time from a gate within Saturn's sphere. I've played with time contraction and expansion, along the lines of the Fotamecus experiment.[9]

---

[8] Seriously though, if you're reading this and it resonates with you the way it resonates with me, I guarantee you're safe. Hermetic magic appeals to people called to Hermeticism. Being called sets you apart from the rest of the world. This confers a certain immunity to a lot of bad shit.

[9] http://www.chaosmatrix.org/library/chaos/rites/fotamec3.html

Perhaps the most useful time experience I've had with Saturn was when I felt overwhelmed and did a rite to create more time in my personal sphere as part of my own kingdom-expansion rite. Things changed almost immediately. I simply had more time to do the things I needed to do, and things seemed to get finished more quickly. Perhaps all that happened was a sense of stress and urgency to meet deadlines vanished. I don't understand what exactly happened, but I found myself on top of things that had been overwhelming a few days before I did the rite.

Saturn spirits can help speed things along. They can help get you appointments that fit into your schedule. They can aid in getting consistently tardy people to show up on time when you need them to.

Just remember they're spirits of the Greater Malefic, and the more malevolent resonance you build up through association with them, the more depressed, slow, and confined you'll feel. Not only that, Saturn spirits also bring death, you know? A death spirit to knock someone off "Pagan Standard Time" is sort of extreme.

## *Wisdom*

Saturn is also the sphere of Wisdom. I touched on that earlier when I mentioned that Mr. Grim knows the beginnings and endings of all things that pass through his sphere. He can make you understand the consequences of your actions in ways you wouldn't normally consider, causing you to make the right decisions in the moment. He can take away the pressures of the moment by extending your personal time to contemplate your situation.

And the neat thing about Saturn wisdom is that it comes without a lot of effort. When you pass through the Gate of Saturn, you will just find yourself becoming wiser. I know the arguments against it, and I understand the arguments against even saying something like, "You don't have to do anything to get results with this magic." No magic is like that, right? And there's no ritual that can just make you wise, right?

Well, the Saturn initiation does.

Besides, you're not doing this rite first. You're starting in Jupiter like I said. Right? Right. So by the time you get here, you'll have passed through all the other Gates, and you'll have built up a lot of experiences in each of the other spheres. I think what happens is that you get a better perspective of your experiences in Saturn, and it puts things into place for you. You can see further in time, and understand the interconnectedness of seemingly separated aspects of existence. You have compassion for your brothers and sisters because you see the shared point of origin. You understand that everything that passes Below passes through this sphere first, and you have a kinship with them. This Wisdom is simply there.

A little bit at a time, you'll find yourself making wise choices. You'll lose weight, gain muscle, finish your projects on time, and reap the rewards in their due time. You'll see how to use your magic to make the changes you desire. Your very desires will form around wise pursuits. Things just get better.

## *Cursing and Hexing*

I know after all the positive aspects of Saturn we've discussed, this part kind of sucks. The reality is that Saturn is pretty evil in its manifestation in people's lives. Whether it's fate manifesting in a Free-Will-Believer, or the slow decay of the flesh, Saturn sucks. Sure, with the Wisdom of Saturn you can come to terms with the bad shit that happens in life, but it still sucks to go through. And really, when you think about what "evil" means to you, you'll find that everything that falls within the spectrum of "evil" is something that sucks to experience.

Saturn is a great place to go to get bad shit to happen. Revenge is a dish best served cold, and there's nothing colder than a blast of the forces of Saturn. It's like someone walking across your grave. You feel it in your bones. It's a fundamental chill.

The thing is, when you pass through the Gate of Saturn, you get that profound wisdom. That usually overrides the desires for hasty vengeance. It lets you put the situation in perspective, and releases you to curse with abandon if it accomplishes your aims, or patiently wait for the inevitable conclusion all things come to regardless of your intervention.

Sometimes passions overcome wisdom, and you go into Saturn all unbalanced and hot, and you conjure up something to end a situation with which you have had enough. Remember I was talking about the mystical aspects of your position during the ritual? If you're all hot and bothered about something when you go conjuring things in Saturn, you leave yourself open to the negative impact of the spirit's influence on your kingdom. Curses that make the curser sick are a good example. I remember reading in Kraig's *Modern Magick* about a Satanist who knew her curses worked when she had something bad happen in her life.

That's bad magic. If you're careful, if you go in cool, evaluate your options, and determine the best course of action in Wisdom, and then afterwards spend time in the Solar sphere, or another sphere that will balance the Saturn influence, any negative ripple in your kingdom from the Work will be dissipated and mitigated.

I would hope you wouldn't curse anyone. It's not nice, and it rarely makes anything better for anyone involved. Like Paracelsus said though, it's the dose that makes the poison. In small doses, that which kills can also cure. And sometimes removing evil is done by performing what looks like evil in other people's eyes.

In my personal practice, I find myself cursing people on average once every three months or so. It's not a regular thing, and I might go six months without cursing anyone, and then find myself cursing two people in a week. It's rare, and it takes a certain combination of ignorance, arrogance, and intent to get me to send evil at anyone. People who are stupid on purpose because they think they're right are just asking for it.

And it's all really subjective. I don't pretend to be an objective force for good in my curses, but I do trust that any curses I place are placed because it is my role in life to place those curses when I see fit. Sometimes people just need a good cursin', and I'm the best magician for the job.

You'll note I don't get into any moral questions here. Ultimately, we do what we want, and we face the consequences. I think that sums it up pretty well, and if you ever curse anyone, you'll understand what I mean.

## Border Expansion

When you do a ritual to expand your Kingdom, after conjuring Cassiel and speaking the Orphic hymn, include something like this:

> *Thou Archangel Cassiel, I ask now for your blessing. Bless me indeed, enlarge my border, and bring me the wisdom to rule within these expanded borders. Keep my Kingdom from all evil, make strong the boundaries and let nothing take away that which has been granted unto me. Let this movement of my limitations not be to my Sorrow, in the name of the Father, son, and Holy Spirit, Amen.*

# Ritual Planning

In the following sections, we'll be going over the basic planning requirements for the performance of the conjuration rites that will take you through the actual establishment of your Kingdom. We start I the sphere of Jupiter, and work our way down through the spheres to the Sphere of the Moon, at which point, if you're ready, we jump back up to the sphere of Saturn to expand the boundaries of our spheres.

## The Schedule

It's possible to go through the seven spheres in seven days, and it's actually a lot of fun. I've done it, and so have several of my friends and colleagues. It can release a lot of power way too quickly though, and it's really not very safe. I mean, when the forces that result in a complete transformation of your life are all moving at once, it can get . . . uhm, not fun. Overwhelming. One might burn out, in fact.

In theory.

As a result, the approach I recommend is paced a little more slowly. If you follow the schedule I lay out below, it will take five weeks to go through all seven spheres. This is still a pretty heavy pace for most folks, and it will completely transform your life.

The table below shows how the schedule will fall on the calendar. You begin in Jupiter on a Thursday, and you finish in Saturn on a Saturday. This schedule gives you about four days of rest between each rite, and a little time to integrate the forces into your sphere and get used to them. At the same time, it doesn't give you enough time to finish materializing the forces you've released. It keeps them in the formative state throughout the whole series of rites. This is useful in making sure the current released in Jupiter is then woven through the other spheres into all aspects of your life.

| Sunday | Monday | Tuesday | Wednesday | Thursday | Friday | Saturday |
|---|---|---|---|---|---|---|
|  |  |  |  | Jupiter |  |  |
|  |  | Mars |  |  |  |  |
| Sun |  |  |  |  | Venus |  |
|  |  |  | Mercury |  |  |  |
|  | Moon |  |  |  |  | (Saturn) |

Note that Saturn is in parentheses. That's because it should be considered optional. You don't need to go to Saturn until you feel completely and fully integrated as the King of your personal Kingdom. You shouldn't go to Saturn until you need to expand the borders of your Kingdom.

Overall, it will take approximately six to eight weeks to perform the rites and have them all begin to really change your life. By the sixth week, you will find that everything has become more intense, obstacles in your way have vanished, and that you've gone through more personal, spiritual, and mental growth than you have in years. By the eighth week, the forces you've released will be materializing and being grounded in your kingdom. You'll find the physical results of the mental and spiritual growth making themselves "real" to you.

It might take a while to get back to a sense of normal. It will happen though. When it does, and you're feeling safe, secure, and happy with how things are going in your life, consider starting the cycle yet again. There is always more to learn in each sphere.

At this point in my life, I am cycling through this schedule almost regularly. It's not as intentional as I'd like it to be, but I find myself in ritual a couple times a week working with one planet or another. Cycling through these spheres is important to Hermeticists. When we conjure these spirits and perform these rites, we are in a sense leaving this material realm and traveling to the seven heavens of the entities. We are ascending, and returning in power.

> 0) *When I entered into the cave, I received the tablet zaradi, which was inscribed, from between the hands of Hermes, in which I discovered these words:*

1) *True, without falsehood, certain, most certain.*
2) *What is above is like what is below, and what is below is like that which is above. To make the miracle of the one thing.*
3) *And as all things were made from contemplation of one, so all things were born from one adaptation.*
4) *Its father is the Sun, its mother is the Moon.*
5) *The wind carried it in its womb, the earth breast fed it.*
6) *It is the father of all 'works of wonder' (Telesmi) in the world.*
6a) *Its power is complete (integra).*
7) *If cast to (turned towards- versa fuerit) earth,*
7a) *it will separate earth from fire, the subtile from the gross.*
8) *With great capacity it ascends from earth to heaven. Again it descends to earth, and takes back the power of the above and the below.*
9) *Thus you will receive the glory of the distinctiveness of the world. All obscurity will flee from you.*
10) *This is the whole most strong strength of all strength, for it overcomes all subtle things, and penetrates all solid things.*
11a) *Thus was the world created.*
12) *From this comes marvelous adaptions of which this is the proceedure.*
13) *Therefore I am called Hermes, because I have three parts of the wisdom of the whole world.*
14) *And complete is what I had to say about the work of the Sun, from the book of Galieni Alfachimi.*

[From Latin in Steele and Singer 1928: 492.]

# Timing

The rites we use are performed on the planetary day in the planetary hour. Calculating the time for the rites is an interesting process.

Planetary hours are periods of time during the day that are ruled by the Seven Planetary Governors.

The idea that each time period is ruled by a planetary spirit can be found most clearly spelled out in Trithemius' *De Septum Secundius*, the Seven Secondary Intelligences. He explains how each of the Planetary Governors rules over a period of time that lasts 354 years, and tracks it back to the beginning of time as he knew it. He shows how the events of each age demonstrate the nature of the ruling spirit.

Similarly, each day of the week is ruled by a planetary governor, and each hour of each day is ruled by a planetary governor. When you are planning planetary magic, the most potent time to perform a ritual is during the Planetary Hour of the Planetary Day. The ruler of the Day has the most influence during his assigned hours of his assigned days. It's easier to establish communications during this time, and the powers he can bring to bear are strongest.

In *The Art of Drawing Spirits into Crystals*, Trithemius provides tables showing which Angels rule each of the Seven Days. Each day is divided into twenty-four hours, and one of the seven Planetary Spirits governs that hour. That means that it's a good time to create planetary talismans, and to conjure the assigned planetary spirits.

The time period covered by a planetary hour is seldom sixty minutes long. Sometimes a planetary hour lasts an hour and twenty minutes, other times only forty-five minutes. This happens because the "hours" are divided into two equal sets of twelve time periods, twelve during the day, and twelve during the night. Due to the rotation of the Earth, summer day hours are longer than summer night hours.

To calculate the time periods represented by a "planetary hour," the magician must figure out how many actual hours there will be during the day, from sunrise to sunset. Find the times of sunrise and sunset, and sum up the total number of hours and minutes that pass between the two. I convert it all to minutes and divide that total by twelve. You do the same for the night hours, measuring the amount of time between sunset and the following sunrise, and dividing that total by twelve.

Once you know the length of time each planetary hour will last, you can begin to chart the planets that rule each hour. Make a numbered list from one to twenty-four down the left side of a page. Write the Start and End Times of each Planetary Hour. Next, you're ready to start adding the planets that rule each hour.

To figure out the first hour angel, you need to know what day it is. Each Day is ruled by one of the seven planets. The first planetary hour is always ruled by the same planet as the planetary day. If today is Friday, Freya-Day, it is ruled by Venus. The first hour of the day is also ruled by Venus. The following list shows the planetary rulers of each day.

# Ritual Planning

- Sunday: The Sun
- Monday: The Moon
- Tuesday: Mars
- Wednesday: Mercury
- Thursday: Jupiter
- Friday: Venus
- Saturday: Saturn

Now you know the planetary ruler of the First Hour of every day. To add the rest, you need to know the Chaldean "Order of the Planets." This is the order that you pass through the planetary spheres on your way from the Sphere of the Fixed Stars to the Sphere of the Earth. For Golden Dawn Kabbalists, it's the Lightning Path beginning with Binah, Saturn. The order is Saturn, Jupiter, Mars, the Sun, Venus, Mercury, and the Moon.

Next to the starting and ending times for the first hour, write the name of the planet that rules the Day. The second hour is ruled by the next planet in the Chaldean Order of the Planets. If today is Friday, the first hour is ruled by Venus, so the second hour will be ruled by Mercury, the third by the Moon, then we go back to the top of the list, so the Fourth is ruled by Saturn, Fifth by Jupiter, the Sixth by Mars, the Seventh by the Sun, and the Eighth by Venus again. The list continues through each of the Planetary Hours until you've got a ruler for all twenty-four time periods.

Note that the Planetary day begins at dawn and doesn't end until Sunrise the following morning. The day doesn't start at midnight. So if I were planning a ritual for Venus today, I could pick any Venus Hour between sunrise today and sunrise tomorrow, even though my calendar thinks it's Saturday starting at midnight. It's not magically Saturday until dawn.

Here's a neat little trick of the universe. Applying the order of the planets to the twenty-four hours of a day always results in the last hour of the day being ruled by the planet that precedes the ruler of the next day. So if tomorrow is Saturday, ruled by Saturn, then the first hour of tomorrow will be the Saturn Hour, so the last planetary hour today will be ruled by Jupiter. It always works out that way. The last hour of a Thursday has to be ruled by

Mercury for the first hour of Friday to be ruled by Venus, and lo and behold, it always is.

The following table provides a quick guide for you to use to figure out the ruler of each hour of the day. You'll still have to figure out the start and finish time for each planetary hour of the day, but this gives you a quick reference:

## Day Hours

| Hours | Sunday | Monday | Tuesday | Wednesday | Thursday | Friday | Saturday |
|---|---|---|---|---|---|---|---|
| 1 | Sun | Moon | Mars | Mercury | Jupiter | Venus | Saturn |
| 2 | Venus | Saturn | Sun | Moon | Mars | Mercury | Jupiter |
| 3 | Mercury | Jupiter | Venus | Saturn | Sun | Moon | Mars |
| 4 | Moon | Mars | Mercury | Jupiter | Venus | Saturn | Sun |
| 5 | Saturn | Sun | Moon | Mars | Mercury | Jupiter | Venus |
| 6 | Jupiter | Venus | Saturn | Sun | Moon | Mars | Mercury |
| 7 | Mars | Mercury | Jupiter | Venus | Saturn | Sun | Moon |
| 8 | Sun | Moon | Mars | Mercury | Jupiter | Venus | Saturn |
| 9 | Venus | Saturn | Sun | Moon | Mars | Mercury | Jupiter |
| 10 | Mercury | Jupiter | Venus | Saturn | Sun | Moon | Mars |
| 11 | Moon | Mars | Mercury | Jupiter | Venus | Saturn | Sun |
| 12 | Saturn | Sun | Moon | Mars | Mercury | Jupiter | Venus |

## Night Hours

| Hours | Sunday | Monday | Tuesday | Wednesday | Thursday | Friday | Saturday |
|---|---|---|---|---|---|---|---|
| 1 | Jupiter | Venus | Saturn | Sun | Moon | Mars | Mercury |
| 2 | Mars | Mercury | Jupiter | Venus | Saturn | Sun | Moon |
| 3 | Sun | Moon | Mars | Mercury | Jupiter | Venus | Saturn |
| 4 | Venus | Saturn | Sun | Moon | Mars | Mercury | Jupiter |
| 5 | Mercury | Jupiter | Venus | Saturn | Sun | Moon | Mars |
| 6 | Moon | Mars | Mercury | Jupiter | Venus | Saturn | Sun |
| 7 | Saturn | Sun | Moon | Mars | Mercury | Jupiter | Venus |
| 8 | Jupiter | Venus | Saturn | Sun | Moon | Mars | Mercury |
| 9 | Mars | Mercury | Jupiter | Venus | Saturn | Sun | Moon |
| 10 | Sun | Moon | Mars | Mercury | Jupiter | Venus | Saturn |
| 11 | Venus | Saturn | Sun | Moon | Mars | Mercury | Jupiter |
| 12 | Mercury | Jupiter | Venus | Saturn | Sun | Moon | Mars |

Now, for those who can figure this out by hand, more power to you! I prefer to use software, such as SolarFire Gold, Timaeus, or ChronosXP. Online, you can find a planetary hour calculator at http://lunarium.co.uk. They also produce an app for smart phones that I use. You simply enter your location, and it displays the current and upcoming planetary hours for your location. It's pretty convenient, and takes a lot less time than figuring out sunrises and sunsets.

Remember, it's the start time of the ritual that matters. It can go on into the next hour if it needs to, as long as it begins within the planetary hour. You can start it one minute before the hour of Saturn begins and still be doing it right. This gives you a lot of flexibility. Which is good, because this is a formal affair.

## A Walkthrough of the Rite

The Conjuration we'll be using is a streamlined version of the Trithemian *Art of Drawing Spirits into Crystals*. By "streamlined," I mean almost completely revamped to reflect my personal understanding of the Hermetic cosmology and my own personally received gnosis. This is a rite that I use regularly. It gets us to the point a lot faster, it conjures up the spirits we need to work with directly, and it doesn't waste a lot of time. It runs best for those who understand the things I laid out in the first sections of this book, but in the limited test runs performed by a super-secret cabal of intermediate magicians in a closed group on Facebook, it worked great.

The ritual consists of three parts. They are the Conjuration of the Archangel, the Oration of the Orphic Hymn of the planet Jupiter, and a period of Meditational Contemplation. Then there's the close out of the rite, and that might deserve to be considered a fourth phase, but it's just... you know, standard magical practice. Magical protocol. Good manners. Common sense.

The conjuration rite begins with a short prayer to the First Father, the Source of us all. In that prayer, we acknowledge where we come from, and where we return. There's a bit about how he resides in eternal darkness, the Divine Darkness that Dionysius the Areopagite talks about, which is followed by the lighting of a single white candle, or the Lamp if you have one dedicated to the purpose in your temple. This candle should be the tallest candle, or placed in a position of honor on your altar or somewhere within the temple.

Following that, we perform a consecration of the temple space. This is an extremely simplified drawing of the Circle of Protection. You start in the East, you trace the circle around clockwise, while saying "I consecrate this ground for our defense in the name of the First Father, His Son and Holy Word the LOGOS, and the Spiritus Mundi who hath formed us all."

Next comes a simplified form of the conjuration of the Headless One taken from the Stele of Jehu. This is the conjuration of the Holy Guardian Angel or Supernatural Assistant who prepares the way between us and the spirits of the Spheres we are contacting.

Then we consecrate the scrying medium, calling upon the animus of the medium itself to keep out evil spirits, or to at least constrain them to speak truth.

Next is the consecration of the incense, which is secretly also the conjuration of Fire. Our Hermetic tradition is the descendent of magical traditions that go back to the Zoroastrians who worshipped fire, and to Heraclitus, who understood the world itself to be an ever-living fire. In our conjuration rite, we conjure a creature of fire to be present and to stand guard, and to govern the effects of the incense we burn, to carry our petitions to the spirits we call, and to ensure that our experiences are true.

Then we conjure the Archangel of the Sphere. This requires the lamen of the spirit and its name, and nothing more.

Then we recite the Orphic Hymn of the god of the planetary sphere. This serves as a Statement of Intent as well as a request for initiation into the sphere, and an empowerment of the magician.

Then we create a Talisman of the planet, combining the correspondences of the spheres of the planet with the seals of the planet's celestial Intelligence and terrestrial Spirit to create a materialization point though which the forces of the planetary spheres can manifest in our lives. This step only needs to be done once, and does not need to be done just to receive the initiation. You can do it at any point, but the sooner you do, the better you'll be able to manifest the forces of the sphere in your material realm.

The final phase of the rite is the period of Meditational Contemplation of the seal of the planet. This provides you with a chance to begin integrating the powers of the Sphere into your own sphere of sensation and experience.

# Ritual Preparation

In the following sections, I've organized the information so you can prepare your altar with the tools that remain the same for each rite (fixed ritual implements), then flip to the specific planet you're working on to get the planet-specific ingredients for the rite (mutable ritual implements). When you've got all your tools and ingredients gathered, you'll be ready to move on to the actual conjuration rite. When you perform the conjuration, you can open the book to the Script section and perform the conjuration and the selected Orphic Hymn, and then put the book down and finish the contemplation portion of the rite.

## The Fixed Ritual Implements

I like to keep the magical rites as simple as possible. That's one of the reasons I like the Trithemian-based system of conjuration we use in this book.

For each rite, you need the following items:

- **Lamp/Tall Candle** – This can be either a consecrated ritual Lamp that you use to represent the First Father in all your rites, or a candle stick that you use for the same purpose. It can also be any tall candle. I use white to represent the purity of the Source, but the First Father exists before any colors.

- **A Scrying Crystal** – This doesn't have to be a crystal ball. Anything with a reflective surface, including a mug of water, can be used.

- **Wand** – The Wand shown below is the one from the *Art of Drawing Spirits into Crystals*, with the words and symbols shown on each side of the wand. Note that you don't have to use a wand; you can also use your index finger, the finger of Jupiter.

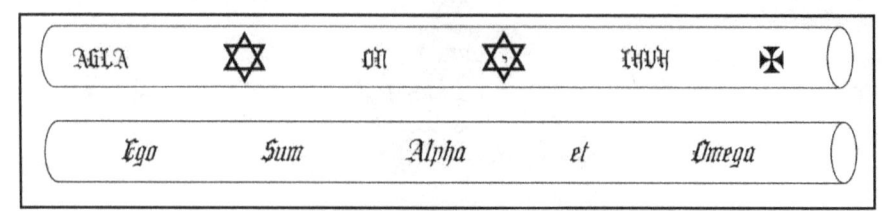

*Figure 1: Trithemian Wand*

- **Incense Burner/Holder** – You can use either stick incense or loose incense. You can use any kind of incense holder you like, just make sure you have somewhere to put the incense during the rite.
- **Table of Practice** – This is your magic circle of conjuration. You can copy the one below by hand onto a piece of blank sketch-pad paper, or a blank white piece of letter paper.

*Figure 2: Table of Practice*

# Ritual Preparation

The following figure shows the basic layout of the fixed implements on your altar. Note that the mutable objects can be arranged however you like and wherever you have room.

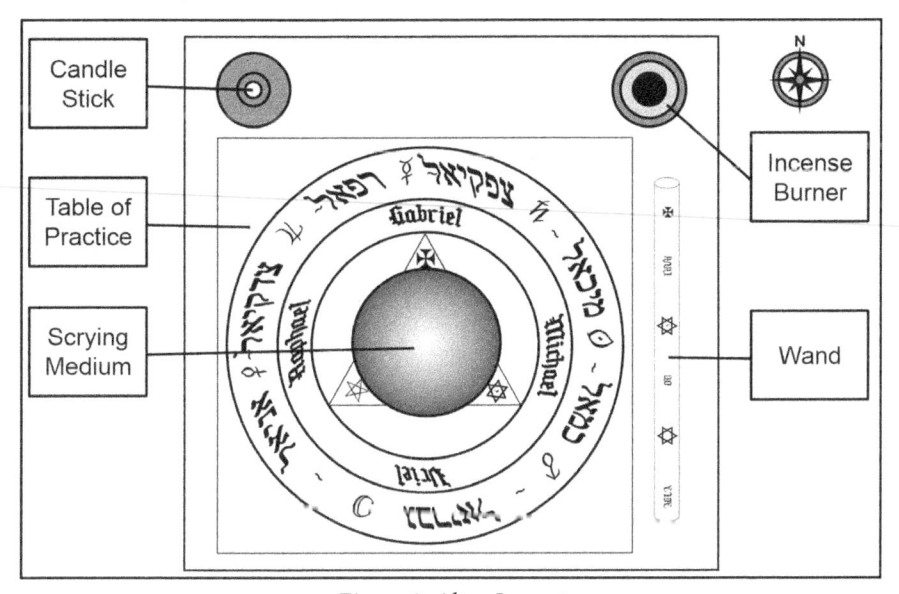

*Figure 3: Altar Layout*

## The Mutable Ritual Implements

In the following sections, I've grouped together the things you'll need for each rite by planet. The idea is that when you're ready to perform the rite, you'll flip to this section, gather your ingredients and draw up the seals and images, and head to your altar to perform the rite.

The following items are specific to each planet and will be the items that change in each rite:

- **Day of the Rite**

- **Attire** – Note that this is optional, but I find it helps sometimes.

- **Alcohol of Choice** – The alcohol of choice is also optional, because not everyone drinks. Some clients have used teas that felt right instead.

- **Cigar of Choice** – This too is optional, as not everyone smokes. I included it originally because the Gents for Jupiter were all about whisky and cigars, and it was fun. But it's not necessary.

- **Planetary Incense** – The incense that I've found works with each of the planets.

- **Mood Music** – Again, an optional element. I often perform rites to a CD of Tibetan singing bowls. It is an effective all-purpose music.

- **Lamen of the Archangel** – A seal of the Archangel that includes its name, its Seal, and some other secret magical words with great meaning that I don't ever explain anywhere.

- **Contemplation Seals** – These are symbols of the planet that you can contemplate after you've said the Orphic Hymn. You can draw them out and gaze upon them with your eyes half-shut while you bask in the forces you've released into your sphere.

## Ritual Preparation

### *Jupiter Conjuration Preparation*

- **Day of the Rite** – Thursday

- **Attire** – The finest suit you own! For the ladies, you will put on your most formal gown and get yourself dressed up to the level that you would feel comfortable in while dining at a white linen restaurant. Now, not all of us are at a point in our lives where we have this kind of formal wear. No worries, just put on the very best clothes you have, the good stuff. Stuff you'd wear to an interview at a prestigious company.

- **Alcohol of Choice** – Your favorite single malt whiskey. Not all of us like whiskey. Substitute a similar beverage of your choice, but make sure it's the very best quality you can afford, or is your favorite thing to drink. Serve it to yourself in the appropriate glassware. Make it special.

- **Cigar of Choice** – Jupiter cigars are any cigar that is mellow and smooth that leaves you feeling almost decadent. Not everyone enjoys a fine cigar. For you poor, poor folks out there who don't appreciate a luxurious smoke, I really don't know what to tell you. Cigars seem pretty Jovial. In a pinch, cigarettes can be substituted, if they're the best ones you have, or cloves if you like those. If you just can't smoke, uhm, I guess you can skip that part. I like having the tobacco left over for use in Jupiter Talismans later, though.

- **Planetary Incense** – Sweet smelling incenses work, as does the Abramelin incense formula. Temple blend are good, and so is basil, mace, and especially lignum aloes. Frankincense will do in a pinch, but you want something sweet and good.

- **Mood Music** – Pick something that symbolizes Jupiter for you. Some have chosen upbeat jazz, others Holst's Planets Op. 32 Jupiter, while others listened to NASA's recordings of the sounds of Jupiter recorded by radio telescopes. I like the "Ode to Joy." It goes well.

- **Lamen of the Archangel** – The Lamen is worn around your neck during the conjuration. You want to draw it out by hand. This makes it more powerful. When you draw out a seal, you are performing a conjuration. You can thread something through the paper to hang it around your neck. Blue thread (blue is the color of Jupiter) would be best, but use what you have.

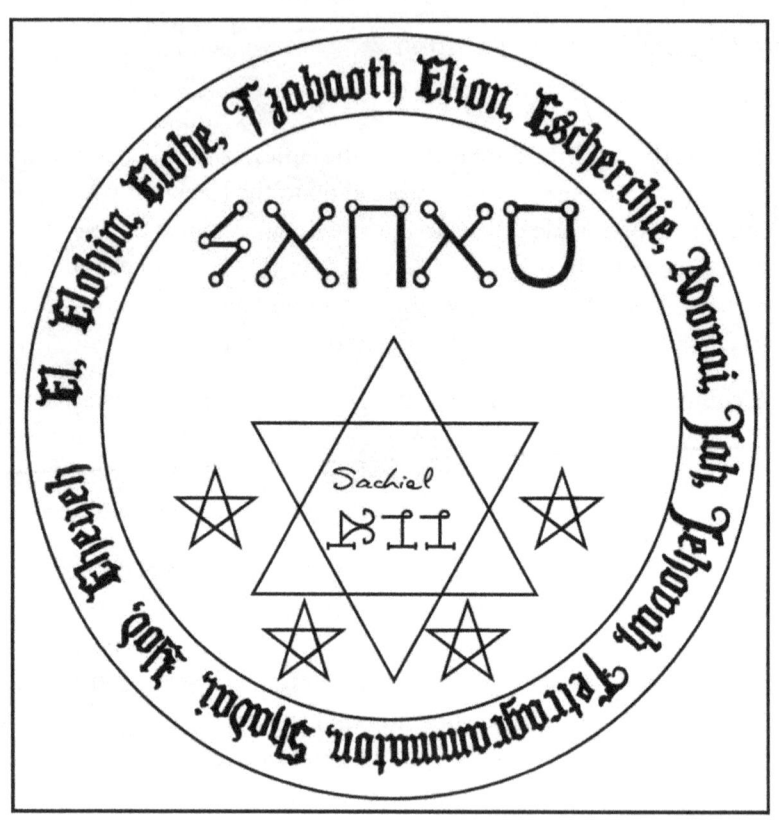

*Figure 4: Lamen of Sachiel*

- Contemplation Seals

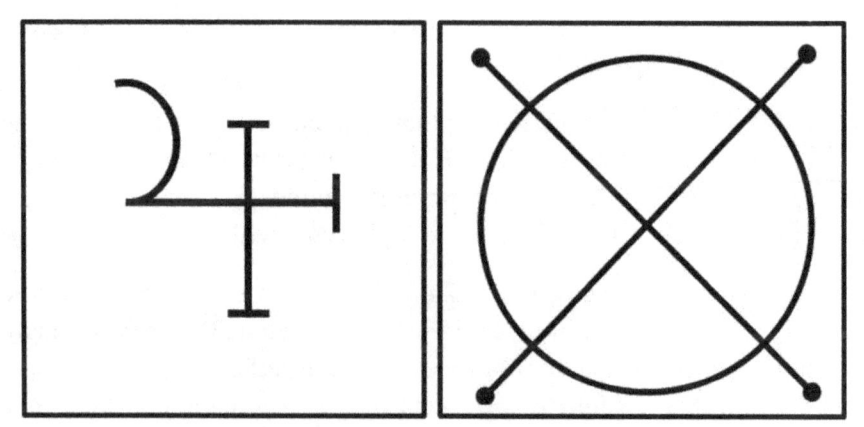

*Figure 5: Contemplation Seals of Jupiter*

## *Mars Conjuration Preparation*

- **Day of the Rite** – Tuesday

- **Attire** – While it would be good to gear up for this, girding yourself with all your daggers and swords and very best Renaissance Fair Royalty outfit, fun even, it is by no means a requirement. If you feel like donning camouflage and a beret and breaking out the KA-BAR spirit knife with AGLAH and the Tetragrammaton acid etched into the grip, by all means! Go for it. Otherwise, this rite can be done in whatever you'd feel comfortable doing a rite in. Robes, formal wear, theme costumery, or just jeans and a t-shirt, anything goes. There is no class of people nor time in history that does not relate to Mars.

- **Alcohol of Choice** – If you drink, I suggest a strong red wine with a high iron content. It can be a sweet wine, like a Port, which I like because it's got more alcohol per volume. It should be strong, whatever it is, and good for celebrating. It should be the kind of drink that makes you horny. Fire Water makes for a good liquor for Mars. It's a 100 proof cinnamon schnapps like thing, but it kicks your ass, hard, and you're left with a strong urge to fuck, or if that's not available, fight. Real bitch of a hangover though, it's like really strong, spicy, cheap vodka. Goldschlager's right out. Period. END of discussion. Forgive yourself if you know what I'm talking about, and if you don't, just move right along.

- **Cigar of Choice** – Cigars should be slightly acidic, leaving a bite on the tongue. Clove cigarettes work too, but they're more in tune with the appeal to Mars in the last bit of the Orphic Hymn, where you ask him to find peace in Venus. Still, it's appropriate for the rite.

- **Planetary Incense** – Cinnamon incense or Abramelin Incense is good for this. Also any "Fire" blends that have frankincense and dragon's blood in it. Good stuff. Especially the Dragon's Blood resin stuff. Early in my magical career, I lived with my parents, who refused to allow me to have incense in my room. I snuck in a cauldron and some incense charcoals, and used black pepper and cinnamon to conjure up the essence of Mars. It worked, and lesson learned was that in most spice aisles in the grocery store are magical resources that work in a pinch. Oh, another lesson learned: Burning black pepper as incense is *THE SUCK*.

Trust me on this one. Don't breathe in the smoke, and a couple friggin' grains go a long ass way. Cough and sneeze central. Lean heavily on ye olde cinnamon.

- **Mood Music** – Music is good too. Holst's "Mars, the Bringer of War" is good. So is a lot of heavy metal music.

- **Lamen of the Archangel** – The Lamen is worn around your neck during the conjuration. You want to draw it out by hand. This makes it more powerful. When you draw out a seal, you are performing a conjuration. You can thread something through the paper to hang it around your neck. Red thread (red is the color of Mars) would be best, but use what you have.

## Ritual Preparation

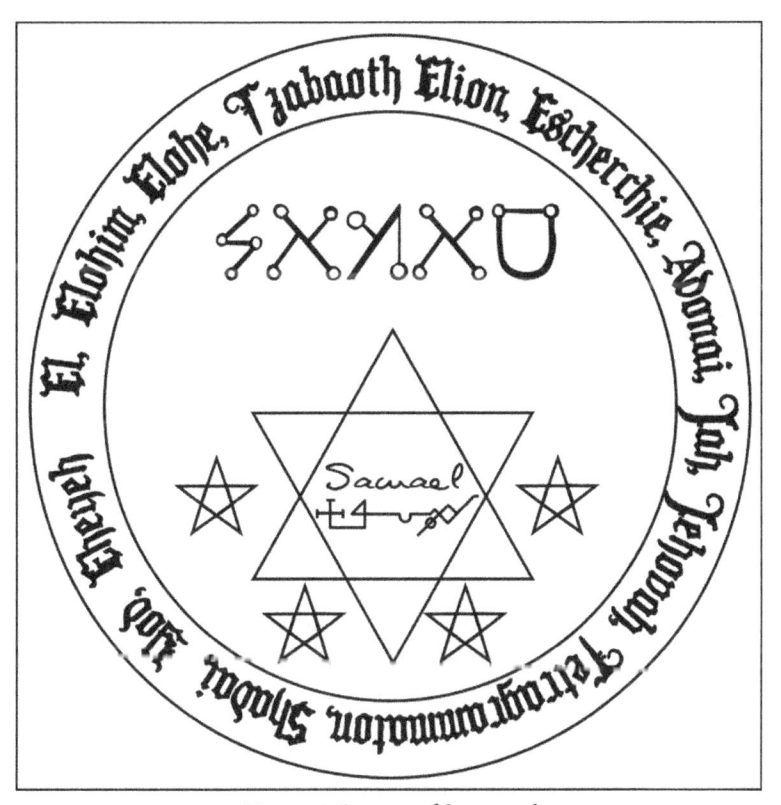

*Figure 6: Lamen of Sammael*

- Contemplation Seals

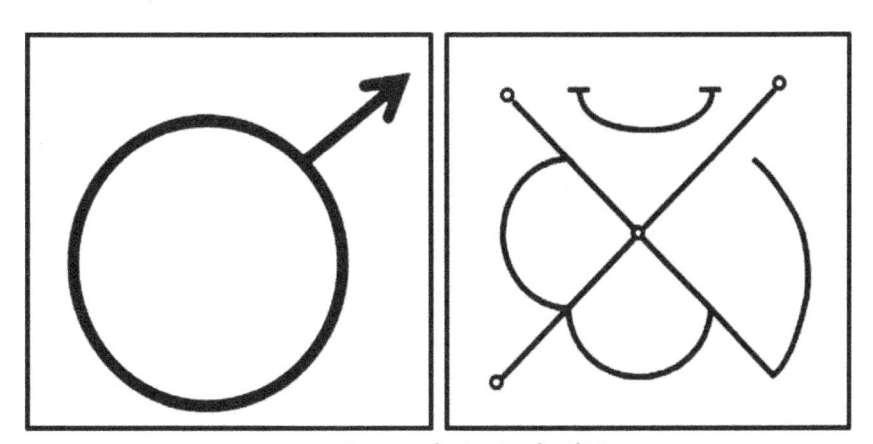

*Figure 7: Contemplation Seals of Mars*

## Solar Conjuration Preparation

- **Day of the Rite** – Sunday

- **Attire** – This rite should be performed with a sense of dignity. The formal attire of Jupiter is not necessary, but you should be wearing clean, nice clothing. Something you wouldn't be ashamed to be seen wearing in public amongst your peers.

- **Alcohol of Choice** – White wines, mead, or mixed drinks work well for the Sun. Sangria is a personal favorite. Margaritas, daiquiris, or piña coladas will work too. "Wines that foam" are also enjoyable here. Some scotches may be appropriate, but they need to be floral on the tongue.

- **Cigar of Choice** – When you choose the appropriate cigar, hold in your mind's eye an image of a sun-drenched field. Smell the wind blowing, feel the heat on your skin. With this in mind, select a cigar that smells complimentary to the image in your mind. When you close your eyes and smell it, it should resonate with that warm image.

- **Planetary Incense** – Frankincense is the best incense for this sphere, in my opinion, but that's just me. The Abramelin incense works great as well here as it does in Mars, perhaps even better.

- **Mood Music** – When choosing a solar music, select something that resonates with the summer. Choose classical music that you would enjoy listening to outside as you sit with your family or friends. It should be warm, and make you feel like moving, whatever genre you select. And fun.

- **Lamen of the Archangel** – The Lamen is worn around your neck during the conjuration. You want to draw it out by hand. This makes it more powerful. When you draw out a seal, you are performing a conjuration. You can thread something through the paper to hang it around your neck. Gold thread or yellow (gold/yellow is the color of the Sun) would be best, but use what you have.

## Ritual Preparation

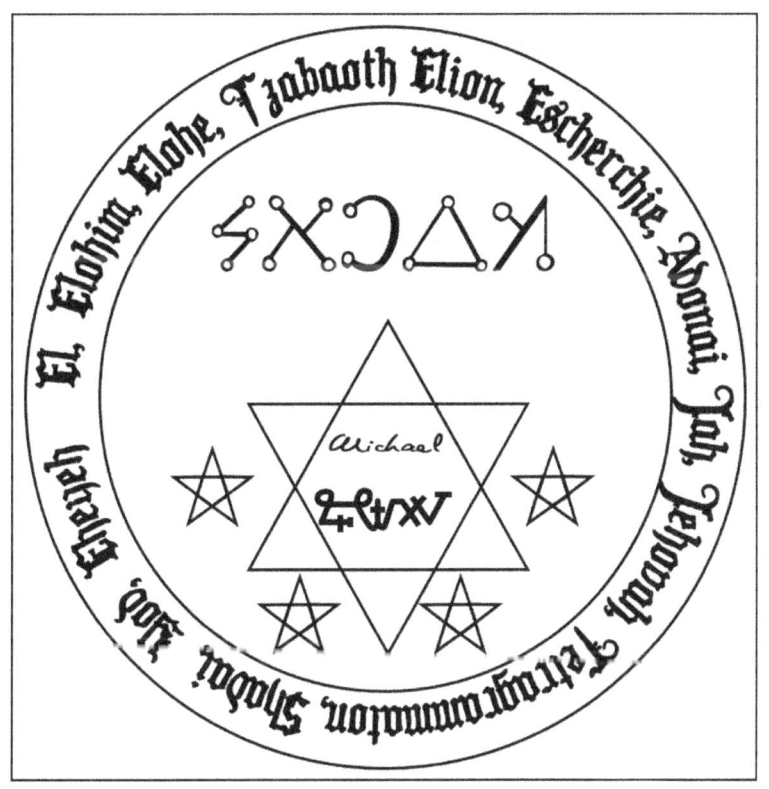

*Figure 8: Lamen of Michael*

- Contemplation Seals

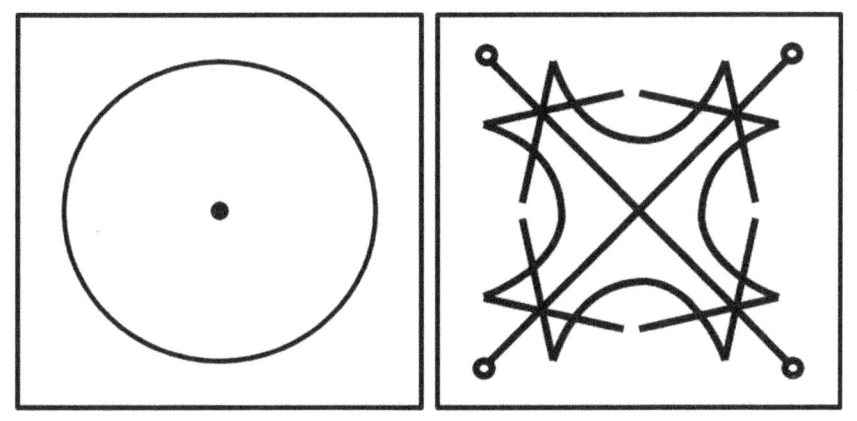

*Figure 9: Contemplation Seals of the Sun*

## *Venus Conjuration Preparation*

- **Day of the Rite** – Friday

- **Attire** – When performing rites of Venus, I like to feel sexy. While for some that might mean wearing very little, or somewhat provocative attire, for me it translates into putting on a decent suit and wearing some nice cologne. I'll get some flowers for the altar space, light some green candles, and pick out some musky "reowr" incense that puts me in the mood.

- **Alcohol of Choice** – For Venus, the liqueurs of love, the sweet and heady wines are all appropriate. Good wines. Good drinks. Drinks that make you feel good about life. The bitter depressing angst-enhancing stuff is right out. And all forms of Mad Dog 20/20 are anathema to Venus.

- **Cigar of Choice** – Venusian cigars should be long and fat, and should bring you pleasure to smoke. Above all, the pleasure is more important than the size. As long as you don't leave the ritual feeling unsatisfied, you've picked the right cigar.[10]

- **Planetary Incense** – For incenses, you want to pick something that smells sweet or floral. Rose and honeysuckle are the scents you want to use as your baseline. Musky scents work too, and Agrippa recommends Sandalwood.

- **Mood Music** – When choosing a Venusian music, pick something romantic, something that puts you in the mood to create or to make love. I like Spanish guitar music, salsa, or anything with a hot Latino beat. Again, Holst's planetary music is always good.

- **Lamen of the Archangel** – The Lamen is worn around your neck during the conjuration. You want to draw it out by hand. This makes it more powerful. When you draw out a seal, you are performing a conjuration. You can thread something through the paper to hang it around your neck. Green thread (green is the color of Venus) would be best, but use what you have.

---

10  It's just a cigar.

## Ritual Preparation

*Figure 10: Lamen of Anael*

- Contemplation Seals

*Figure 11: Contemplation Seals of Venus*

## *Mercury Conjuration Preparation*

- **Day of the Rite** – Wednesday

- **Attire** – For Mercurial rites, there is no particularly specific attire that puts me in a mercurial mood. I write in whatever I happen to be wearing, whether it's business casual at my day job, or in shorts and a t-shirt at home. In picking out the types of attire for these rites, I try to think of what would be appropriate for performing actions that are related to the things the planet rules.

- **Alcohol of Choice** – For Mercury, any type of alcoholic beverage that makes you cerebral would be appropriate. Blended whiskeys, like Cutty Sark, work for me. So do red wines, and white wines. Anything that has a loquacious effect would be appropriate. I associate Mercurial beverages with crisp and clean aftertastes, something that doesn't linger on the palate, and something that aids in the flow of communication without taking your attention off what you're talking about.

- **Cigar of Choice** – Mercurial cigars should be thin and crisp. They should have an acrid or metallic scent. Imported cigarettes, clove cigarettes, and hand rolled smokes work really well. I like Drum tobacco for Mercury rites, personally, and there's plenty of loose tobacco available for distribution when you're done. Pipe blends would also be appropriate, tapping into the mixed nature of Mercurial substances.

- **Planetary Incense** – For incenses, you want to pick something that smells sweet or floral. Rose and honeysuckle are the scents you want to use as your baseline. Musky scents work too, and Agrippa recommends Sandalwood.

- **Mood Music** – When choosing a Mercurial music, pick something with a quick tempo or with intellectual lyrics. Techno and techno-trance is good stuff. I also have been enjoying Dub Step for various rites lately. And yet again, Holst's planetary music is always good.

- **Lamen of the Archangel** – The Lamen is worn around your neck during the conjuration. You want to draw it out by hand. This makes it more powerful. When you draw out a seal, you are performing a conjuration. You can thread something through the paper to hang it around your neck. Silver thread (silver is the color of Mercury) would be best, but use what you have.

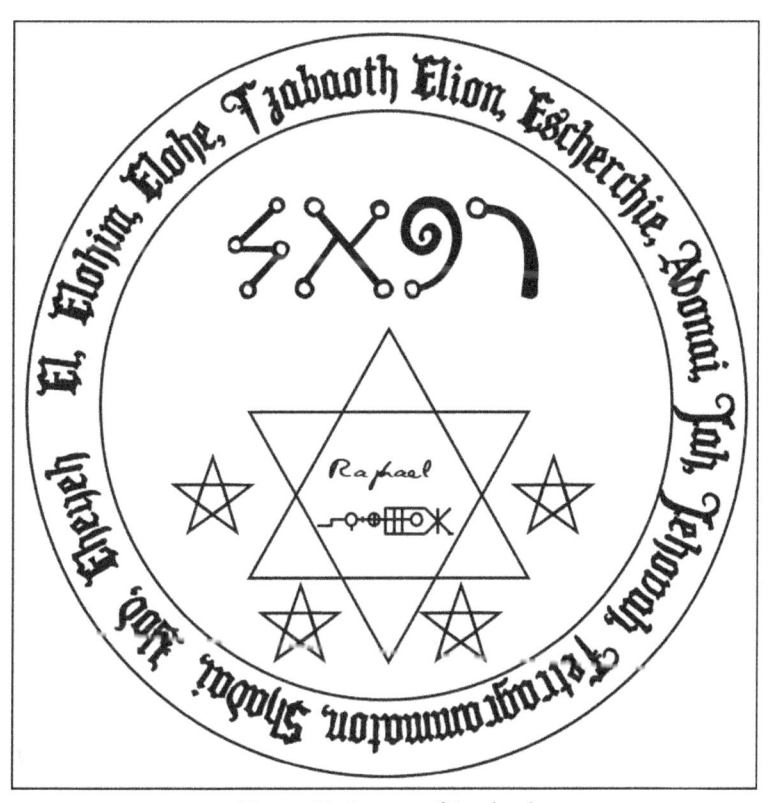

*Figure 12: Lamen of Raphael*

- Contemplation Seals

*Figure 13: Contemplation Seals of Mercury*

## Lunar Conjuration Preparation

- **Day of the Rite** – Monday

- **Attire** – For the Lunar rite, you should dress in something very comfortable, something that breathes well while you're wearing it. Your attire should be light, diaphanous, and flowing. There should be nothing tight or constrictive on you. Robes are good for Lunar rites, as long as they leave you feeling free to move around.

- **Alcohol of Choice** – For the alcoholic beverage of the Moon, I suggest something like absinthe. Mead is also good, and the white wines that are delicious with a hint of apples or pears when you drink them.

- **Cigar of Choice** – Lunar cigars . . . well, there really aren't any that spring to mind. I stick with Montecristos, Reserva Negra for my Lunar rites.

- **Planetary Incense** – For incenses, the traditional sources advise camphor, jasmine, willow, and copal. I like jasmine best, and lavender works well too. Verbena is a good standby too, though it doesn't smell very good burning. Anything that reminds you of a dream when you smell it is good. Opium. Definitely opium.

- **Mood Music** – When choosing a Lunar music, I like something with a nice slow rhythm, something smooth and dreamy. Anything by the Cowboy Junkies puts me in the right mood, and a lot of the more instrumental work by Pink Floyd, specifically the *Wish You Were Here* album is good for me. You want something that is transcendent, that takes you up into a dreamy state of mind, but something that doesn't suck you into it to the point where you can't pay attention to what you're doing. And yet again, Holst's planetary music is always good.

- **Lamen of the Archangel** – The Lamen is worn around your neck during the conjuration. You want to draw it out by hand. This makes it more powerful. When you draw out a seal, you are performing a conjuration. You can thread something through the paper to hang it around your neck. Purple thread (purple is the color of the moon) would be best, but use what you have.

## Ritual Preparation

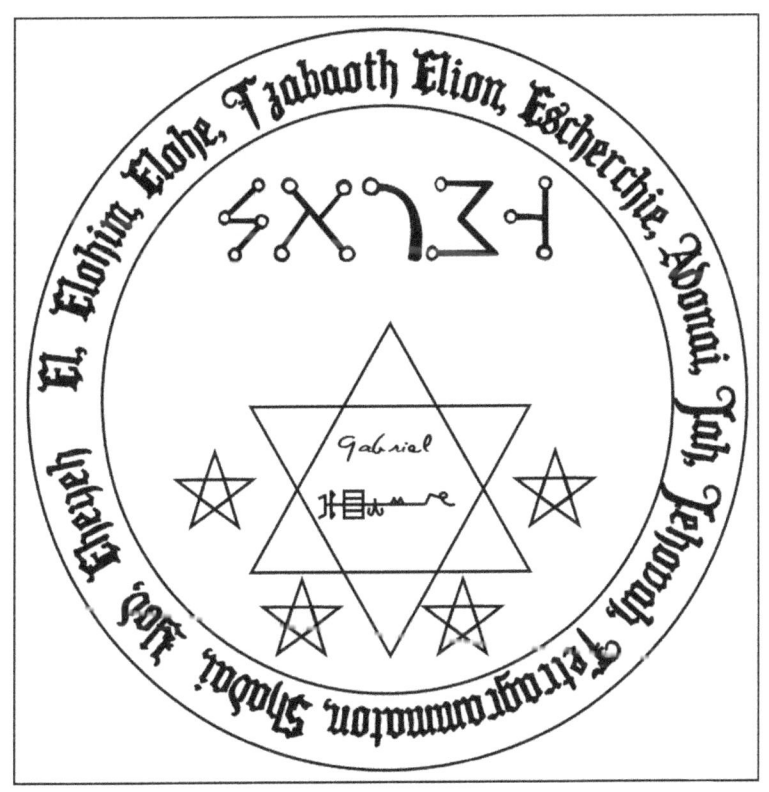

*Figure 14: Lamen of Gabriel*

- Contemplation Seals

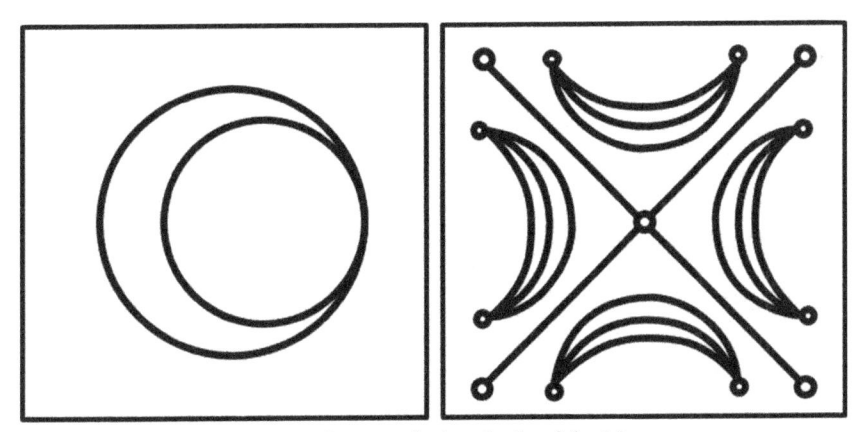

*Figure 15: Contemplation Seals of the Moon*

-109-

## Saturn Conjuration Preparation

- **Day of the Rite** – Saturday

- **Attire** – This rite should be performed with a sense of solemnity. In picking out the appropriate clothing for the ritual, remember that anything you would wear to a funeral works well. Black or dark grey colors work best in my opinion. You should pick something on the formal side of things.

- **Alcohol of Choice** – Dark red, slightly sweet wines with full bodies are best for this sphere. Ports and aperitifs are also appropriate. I suspect Jägermeister would work as well, and the darker, heavier beers.

- **Cigar of Choice** – In selecting a Saturnine cigar, the obvious choices come in a Madura wrapper. You're looking for something thick and heavy, pungent. Someone once described a cigar I was considering buying using the phrase "elephant dung." While it was funny at the time, it didn't really smell like elephant dung, but that's sort of pretty close. Like a full bodied wine, the scent of a Saturnine cigar will reveal depth as you savor its aroma. It will feel subterranean, earthy.

- **Planetary Incense** – The scents of Saturn incense listed in the traditional tomes I find are generally unsuited for indoor use. Asafetida, for example. Sulfur. "Dark and unpleasant odors." Poppy seed works better for me, though it's not that great smelling. Myrrh is also appropriate.

- **Mood Music** – When choosing Saturnine music, I personally prefer the somber classical genre, specifically Holst's "Saturn." Slow ponderous music that elicits a deeply profound state of awareness is always in keeping with this sphere. Some techno/trance can work well. It needs to be something you can feel in your bones, something that you never will grow tired of hearing because it expresses a fundamental truth.

- **Lamen of the Archangel** – The Lamen is worn around your neck during the conjuration. You want to draw it out by hand. This makes it more powerful. When you draw out a seal, you are performing a conjuration. You can thread something through the paper to hang it around your neck. Black thread (black is the color of Saturn) would be best, but use what you have.

# Ritual Preparation

*Figure 16: Lamen of Anael*

- Contemplation Seals

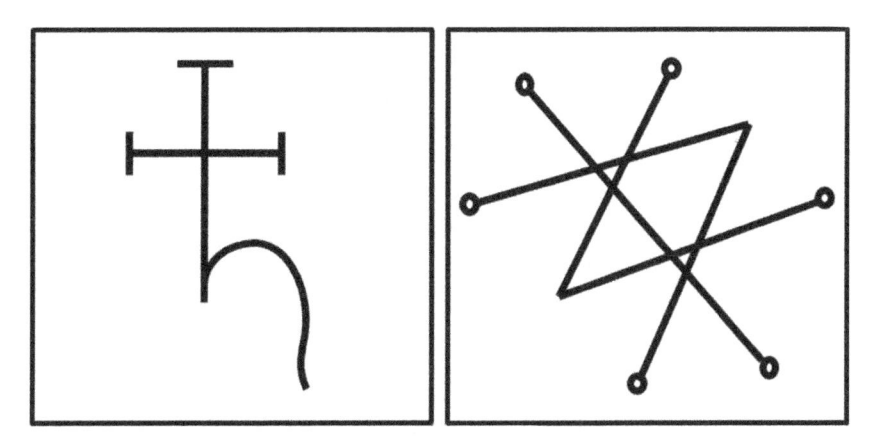

*Figure 17: Contemplation Seals of Saturn*

# The Script

To begin, say the following prayer:

> *First Father, source of all Light, who yet sits in absolute and eternal darkness, you who have expressed through your Word all that is, you who, with the Loving Spiritus Mundi, have shaped me in your image as divine creator god, I call upon you now to bless and consecrate these rites.*

[Light a white candle.]
Trace out a circle beginning in the East, and say:

> *I consecrate this ground for our defense, in the name of the Father, Son, and Holy Spirit.*

Face the North.
Say the following Words:

*AŌTH ABRAŌTH BASYM ISAK SABAŌTH IAŌ.*

As you speak the words aloud, visualize them written across your forehead, stretching from one temple to the other. Let these words crown you, and then say:

> *Subject to me all daimons, so that every daimon, whether heavenly or aerial or earthly or subterranean or terrestrial or aquatic, might be obedient to me and every enchantment and scourge which is from God.*

Then say,

> *Thou supernatural assistant, ever present friend and guide, prepare now the way between myself and the sphere of Mercury, and its Intelligences. Prepare a feast for those entities we shall call, and make straight the way between us.*

Bless the scrying medium:

> *Oh inanimate creature of God, be sanctified and consecrated, and blessed to this purpose, that no evil fantasy may appear in you; or, if they do, that they may be constrained to speak intelligibly, and truly, and without the least ambiguity, for Christ's sake. Amen.*

Bless the incense:

> *I conjure thee, oh thou creature of fire! by him who created all things both in heaven and earth, and in the sea, and in every other place whatsoever, that you cast away every phantasm from you, that no hurt whatsoever shall be done in any thing. Bless, oh Lord, this creature of fire, and sanctify it that it may be blessed, and that you may fill me up with the power and virtue of their odors; so neither any enemy, nor any false imagination may enter into this space; through our Lord Jesus Christ. Amen.*

Conjure the Archangel of the Sphere:

> *"In the name of the blessed and holy Trinity, I conjure you, you strong mighty angel [Angel Name], that if it is the divine will of Tetragrammaton, the Holy God, the Father, that you take the shape that best reflects your celestial nature, and appear here in this crystal, to the glory and honor of his divine Majesty, who lives and reigns, world without end. Amen.*
>
> *"Lord, your will be done on earth, as it is in heaven; -- make clean my heart within me, and take not your Holy Spirit from me.*
>
> *"O Lord, by your name I have called him, suffer him to minister unto me. And that all things may work together for your*

*honor and glory, to whom, with you, the Son and blessed Spirit are ascribed all might, majesty and dominion. Amen"*

"*Oh, Lord! thank you for the hearing of my prayer, and thank you for allowing your spirit to appear unto me. Amen.*"

Recite the Orphic Hymn.

# The Orphic Hymn to Jupiter

Recite the following Hymn to Jupiter:

> *O Jove much-honoured, Jove supremely great,*
> *To thee our holy rites we consecrate,*
> *Our prayers and expiations, king divine,*
> *For all things round thy head exalted shine.*
> *The earth is thine, and mountains swelling high,*
> *The sea profound, and all within the sky.*
> *Saturnian king, descending from above,*
> *Magnanimous, commanding, sceptred Jove;*
> *All-parent, principle and end of all,*
> *Whose power almighty, shakes this earthly ball;*
> *Even Nature trembles at thy mighty nod,*
> *Loud-sounding, armed with lightning, thundering God.*
> *Source of abundance, purifying king,*
> *O various-formed from whom all natures spring;*
> *Propitious hear my prayer, give blameless health,*
> *With peace divine, and necessary wealth.*

# The Orphic Hymn to Mars

Recite the following Hymn to Mars:

> *Magnanimous, unconquer'd, boistrous Mars,*
> *In darts rejoicing, and in bloody wars*
> *Fierce and untam'd, whose mighty pow'r can make*
> *The strongest walls from their foundations shake:*
> *Mortal destroying king, defil'd with gore,*
> *Pleas'd with war's dreadful and tumultuous roar:*

*Thee, human blood, and swords, and spears delight,*
*And the dire ruin of mad savage fight.*
*Stay, furious contests, and avenging strife,*
*Whose works with woe, embitter human life;*
*To lovely Venus, and to Bacchus yield,*
*To Ceres give the weapons of the field;*
*Encourage peace, to gentle works inclin'd,*
*And give abundance, with benignant mind.*

## The Orphic Hymn to the Sun
Recite the following Hymn to the Sun:

*HEAR golden Titan, whose eternal eye*
*With broad survey, illumines all the sky.*
*Self-born, unwearied in diffusing light,*
*And to all eyes the mirror of delight:*
*Lord of the seasons, with thy fiery car*
*And leaping coursers, beaming light from far:*
*With thy right hand the source of morning light,*
*And with thy left the father of the night.*
*Agile and vigorous, venerable Sun,*
*Fiery and bright around the heavens you run.*
*Foe to the wicked, but the good man's guide,*
*O'er all his steps propitious you preside:*
*With various founding, golden lyre, 'tis mine*
*To fill the world with harmony divine.*
*Father of ages, guide of prosperous deeds,*
*The world's commander, borne by lucid steeds,*
*Immortal Jove, all-searching, bearing light,*
*Source of existence, pure and fiery bright*
*Bearer of fruit, almighty lord of years,*
*Agile and warm, whom every power reveres.*
*Great eye of Nature and the starry skies,*
*Doomed with immortal flames to set and rise*
*Dispensing justice, lover of the stream,*
*The world's great despot, and over all supreme.*
*Faithful defender, and the eye of right,*

*Of steeds the ruler, and of life the light:*
*With founding whip four fiery steeds you guide,*
*When in the car of day you glorious ride.*
*Propitious on these mystic labours shine,*
*And bless thy supplicants with a life divine.*

# The Orphic Hymn to Venus
Recite the following Hymn to Venus:

*HEAVENLY, illustrious, laughter-loving queen,*
*Sea-born, night-loving, of an awful mien;*
*Crafty, from whom necessity first came,*
*Producing, nightly, all-connecting dame:*
*Tis thine the world with harmony to join,*
*For all things spring from thee, O power divine.*
*The triple Fates are ruled by thy decree,*
*And all productions yield alike to thee:*
*Whatever the heavens, encircling all contain,*
*Earth fruit-producing, and the stormy main,*
*Thy sway confesses, and obeys thy nod,*
*Awful attendant of the brumal God:*
*Goddess of marriage, charming to the sight,*
*Mother of Loves, whom banquetings delight;*
*Source of persuasion, secret, favouring queen,*
*Illustrious born, apparent and unseen:*
*Spousal, lupercal, and to men inclined,*
*Prolific, most-desired, life-giving, kind:*
*Great sceptre-bearer of the Gods, tis thine,*
*Mortals in necessary bands to join;*
*And every tribe of savage monsters dire*
*In magic chains to bind, thro mad desire.*
*Come, Cyprus-born, and to my prayer incline,*
*Whether exalted in the heavens you shine,*
*Or pleased in Syrias temple to preside,*
*Or over the Egyptian plains thy car to guide,*
*Fashioned of gold; and near its sacred flood,*
*Fertile and famed to fix thy blest abode;*

*Or if rejoicing in the azure shores,*
*Near where the sea with foaming billows roars,*
*The circling choirs of mortals, thy delight,*
*Or beauteous nymphs, with eyes cerulean bright,*
*Pleased by the dusty banks renowned of old,*
*To drive thy rapid, two-yoked car of gold;*
*Or if in Cyprus with thy mother fair,*
*Where married females praise thee every year,*
*And beauteous virgins in the chorus join,*
*Adonis pure to sing and thee divine;*
*Come, all-attractive to my prayer inclined,*
*For thee, I call, with holy, reverent mind.*

# The Orphic Hymn to Mercury

Recite the following Hymn to Mercury:

*Hermes, draw near, and to my prayer incline,*
*Angel of Jove, and Maia's son divine;*
*Studious of contests, ruler of mankind,*
*With heart almighty, and a prudent mind.*
*Celestial messenger, of various skill,*
*Whose powerful arts could watchful Argus kill:*
*With winged feet, tis thine thro air to course,*
*O friend of man, and prophet of discourse:*
*Great life-supporter, to rejoice is thine,*
*In arts gymnastic, and in fraud divine:*
*With power endued all language to explain,*
*Of care the loosener, and the source of gain.*
*Whose hand contains of blameless peace the rod,*
*Corucian, blessed, profitable God;*
*Of various speech, whose aid in works we find,*
*And in necessities to mortals kind:*
*Dire weapon of the tongue, which men revere,*
*Be present, Hermes, and thy suppliant hear;*
*Assist my works, conclude my life with peace,*
*Give graceful speech, and me memory's increase.*

## THE ORPHIC HYMN TO THE MOON
Recite the following Hymn to the Moon:

> *Hear, Goddess queen, diffusing silver light,*
> *Bull-horned and wandering thro the gloom of Night.*
> *With stars surrounded, and with circuit wide*
> *Nights torch extending, thro the heavens you ride:*
> *Female and Male with borrowed rays you shine,*
> *And now full-orbed, now tending to decline.*
> *Mother of ages, fruit-producing Moon,*
> *Whose amber orb makes Nights reflected noon:*
> *Lover of horses, splendid, queen of Night,*
> *All-seeing power bedecked with starry light.*
> *Lover of vigilance, the foe of strife,*
> *In peace rejoicing, and a prudent life:*
> *Fair lamp of Night, its ornament and friend,*
> *Who gives to Natures works their destined end.*
> *Queen of the stars, all-wife Diana hail!*
> *Decked with a graceful robe and shining veil;*
> *Come, blessed Goddess, prudent, starry, bright,*
> *Come moony-lamp with chaste and splendid light,*
> *Shine on these sacred rites with prosperous rays,*
> *And pleased accept thy suppliants mystic praise.*

## THE ORPHIC HYMN TO SATURN
Recite the following Hymn to Saturn:

> *Ethereal father, mighty Titan, hear,*
> *Great fire of Gods and men, whom all revere:*
> *Endowed with various council, pure and strong,*
> *To whom perfection and decrease belong.*
> *Consumed by thee all forms that hourly die,*
> *By thee restored, their former place supply;*
> *The world immense in everlasting chains,*
> *Strong and ineffable thy power contains*
> *Father of vast eternity, divine,*
> *O mighty Saturn, various speech is thine:*

*Blossom of earth and of the starry skies,*
*Husband of Rhea, and Prometheus wife.*
*Obstetric Nature, venerable root,*
*From which the various forms of being shoot;*
*No parts peculiar can thy power enclose,*
*Diffused thro' all, from which the world arose,*
*O, best of beings, of a subtle mind,*
*Propitious hear to holy prayers inclined;*
*The sacred rites benevolent attend,*
*And grant a blameless life, a blessed end.*

## CLOSEOUT

When you're finished with the contemplation of the Seal of Jupiter, it's time to say goodbye to the Archangel.

> "You great and mighty spirit, as you came in peace and in the name of the ever blessed and righteous Trinity, you may now depart in this same name, and return when I call you in his name to whom every knee bows down. Fare well, [Angel Name]; peace be between us, through our blessed Lord Jesus Christ. Amen."

The spirit will then leave. Say:

> "To God the Father, eternal Spirit, fountain of Light, the Son, and Holy Ghost, be all honor and glory, world without end. Amen."

After you've given the license to depart, take your favorite drink outside, and dig a little hole in the dirt. Pour out your drink into the Earth while saying, "[Planet Name], I dedicate this to you and your spirits in the Elemental World. Empower them, that they make work on my behalf."

If it's alcoholic, ignite it. (Safely; don't start a wildfire in Texas or California doing Magic. BAD FORM. If you can't be safe, don't do it. It's optional.)

# Talismans

This section provides the basic instructions required to create a talisman for each of the Planets. The purpose of creating such a talisman is to create a physical link to each of the planetary spheres and the spirits thereof so they have a "body" through which to work in your personal sphere.

Much of this section has appeared as the *Rufus Opus Talisman Maintenance and Operations Manual*. What can I say, I'm a technical writer. Titles . . . meh. I've included the ingredients and the consecration rites for each of the planets here in this section. You don't have to make the talismans to benefit from the rites, which is why this is one of the final chapters of the book. It helps, but it is not necessary.

When you do get around to making these talismans, you'll perform the ritual as described in chapters 13 and 14, but after the Orphic hymn you will insert the consecration of the ingredients of the talismans, put together the ingredients creating the talisman, and then consecrate it. Then you'll finish with the contemplation section of the rite.

In the following sections, we'll be going over the fundamental Hermetic features of talismans, and the best ways to maximize their influence in your life. By creating this magical item, you will have entered into a relationship with the spirit of the item, and by cultivating this relationship and performing regular maintenance, you will enjoy a long and fruitful friendship.

## The Nature of Talismans

In Hermetics, we learn that everything that exists is made of the soul of the Spiritus Mundi, woven together by the elementals, and reflecting a specific idea from the Mind of God. Hermetic animism sees all things as not only being constructed of soul, but having its own soul that can be contacted and communed with. Genius Loci are more commonly referred to manifestations of this feature of existence, but everything from the streams, trees, and rocks to the jeans, tees, and socks you wear have a soul that can be worked with Hermetically. They are your distant cousins, made of the same star stuff as you are, in different proportions.

This includes the Talisman. A Talisman is partially created, partially called. The material base is made of things that share in the occult virtues the magician is putting together to draw down through the principles of similitude. The spirits he is calling through this material base are the spirits who revealed to the magician how to create the talisman in the first place. In other words, a magician may conjure the Intelligence of Mercury to grant initiation into its Sphere. As a result, the magician receives revelations of the qualities of the sphere, including spirit names and traits, ingredients, seals, shapes, and powers. Forces of the planet are released into the sphere of the magician, empowering him in Mercurial Manifestation. The instruction he received and the power resonating within him lead him to encapsulate what is represented in a form, a talisman. The spirits in resonance with the intent, who brought about the initiation in the first place, are now available to aid him in his assigned tasks related to their sphere.

## *Types of Talismans*

A talisman can be made of a single metal, a gemstone, a finely crafted piece of jewelry, or a rough bag of herbs and stones. It can be a vial of fluid or molded clay. It can be a living plant or animal, or the necrotic bio-matter of the same. Talismans can be actively used implements, like elemental tools (wands, daggers, chalices and pentacles), or passive forces present in more subtle ways, like paintings made over seals of spirits, or incorporating Hermetic imagery directly.

There are many forms of maintenance techniques available, and the best should be chosen for your talisman. You can immerse a metal talisman in a liquid offering, but doing so to a mojo bag could leach away the forces it represents. In determining the proper maintenance for your talisman, consider how long you want it to last and take appropriate measures.

## Talismanic Maintenance

By learning to appreciate the talisman as a physical representation of an entity, you are creating a framework of communication with the entity it represents. You'll be able to conjure them quickly by lighting a candle, speaking a prayer, or making an offering of some other kind that affects the talisman. Baptisms of holy water, the pouring of libations, the kindling of a flame, the oration of a hymn are all methods of establishing and maintaining your relationship with the spirits represented by the talisman.

Note we're talking about "offerings," but this should not be confused with worship. You are no more worshipping a talisman by pouring a shot of fine whiskey over it than you are worshipping your telephone by dialing it. In case you were concerned about that pesky "worship of false idols" bit.

## *Initial Consecration: Activation of the Talisman*

If you've purchased the talisman from a magician who knows what he's doing, chances are good that the talisman you have has been activated by performing an official first consecration of the materials gathered and the symbols inscribed.

If you're not sure the creator of the talisman knows his ass from a hole in the ground, or if you have created it yourself, then you'll need to activate the forces it represents yourself.

Most of my talismans have direct planetary correspondences. Consequently, I'm able to time my consecrations relatively easily by planetary day and hour. There are apps and widgets and web sites and calculators online that can tell you exactly when the most convenient time to do a ritual would be. I also am quite comfortable with the ease of the planetary magic provided through the rites detailed in the *Modern Angelic Grimoire*. For those not comfortable with Angelic Magic, the Orphic Hymns to the Planets provide a convenient method of consecrating anything planetary in a quick and easy way.

For talismans that are not directly planetary by nature, I'm left with identifying the spirit or effect I'm aiming for as best as I can. Naming the talisman helps in these instances, treating it like a little golem and breathing life into it as part of the ritual are important.

## *Initial Consecration Rite: Angelic Planetary Method*

When using the *Modern Angelic Grimoire*, or something similar that results in the conjuration of the Archangel or Planetary Intelligence or Olympik Spirit, the most effort you will expend on this is the writing of an appropriate Charge to the Spirit. You conjure the spirit and grant it the license to depart as you normally would, but while it's present, you explain what you want the talisman to accomplish, and have the spirit grant its blessing.

The initial consecration charge to the spirit should include the following:

- The reason you created it, a specific explanation of what you want the talisman to accomplish for you.

- A request for consecration. This sets the item apart and makes it holy to accomplish its intent within the material realm.

- A request for empowerment. If you are working with a planetary talisman that has a specific, named entity assigned to operate through it, you request that spirit be empowered to accomplish the intent of the talisman.

- The name of the person you are consecrating the talisman for, if it's not for yourself.

An example from a recent talisman consecration went something like this:

> *Iophial I ask that you bring to this place in this time Hasmial, Spirit of the Sphere of Jupiter. In the name of El, I conjure thee Hasmial, by thy name and thy seal I conjure thee. Come now to this place.*
>
> *Iophial, I bring before you this talisman of the Sphere of Jupiter for consecration and empowerment. Consecrate it to bring to [client name] the forces of the sphere of Jupiter, that the graces of thy sphere pour out upon them. Teach them the ways of right rulership, and grant them the wealth and power they require to accomplish their tasks. Grant also the wisdom to manage these forces.*
>
> *Shepherd the graces through the celestial realms, Iophial, and guide them to manifestation, Hasmial. Let your powers be felt and known by [client name], that they may respond to the opportunities you bring. Bless them with wisdom and grace.*

## *Scheduled Maintenance*

Talismans, like children, require a steady diet to be healthy, effective, and to continue to grow in strength and influence. When you are actively working with the forces of the talisman, you should feed it on a monthly basis. Weekly is better for rapid growth and activation, but it can be overkill with talismans that are providing an ongoing effect.

Also, if you have a talisman that you carry with you daily, every time you put it on or put it in your pocket, you are "feeding" it a little bit. With these kinds of talismans, you can hold off on a formal feeding rite for as long as three months.

Talismans "eat" offerings made to the spirits they represent. A typical way to feed and maintain a talisman is through consecrated candle magic. Dedicate an appropriately colored candle (white if you don't have the right color) to the Intelligence of the planet(s) that is the primary force of the talisman. This can be done with a full conjuration and consecration ritual over the candles, but it's usually easier for me to use a simple oration.

Place the candles on your altar, point your finger or hand at the candles, and say:

> *[Intelligence Name(s)] of the sphere of [Sphere name(s)], I conjure you to consecrate these candles to your sphere. Let all that is illuminated by their flames receive the powers of your sphere, in the name of the Father, son, and Holy Spirit, Amen.*

A similar prayer may be made over anything you offer to the spirits of the talismans.

With a candle offering, light the candle and say something like:

> *As the light of this candle falls upon you, receive and incorporate the powers of the sphere of [Sphere name]. Be made strong and mighty to accomplish [statement of intent].*

This is the basic form of the prayer you should say while performing a maintenance rite. It's short and simple and to the point. If you prefer something more robust, you can embellish it as you see fit. Keep flowery phrases in keeping with the forces you're working with. You wouldn't recite Shakespeare to migrant workers, nor tell dirty jokes to state dignitaries.

Place the talisman where the light of the candle will fall on it, and let it absorb the powers throughout the planetary hour you are working within. It's okay to start late, and it's okay to go over into the next hour if need be. Just don't start early. Do let your talisman sit in the light for at least an hour.

## *Other Forms of Maintenance*

Another form of consecration uses Suffumigation instead or in addition to the candle. This method involves burning sacred mixtures that have also been consecrated over an incense coal while speaking the prayer of empowerment. The talisman is passed through the smoke for the duration of the prayer.

Libations can be offered as well. You can pour a drink, like whiskey or rum, directly on the talisman, immerse the talisman in it, or simply dedicate the drink to the spirit of the talisman, let it sit near it for a while, and then pour it out into the earth. The libation should be consecrated appropriately ahead of time.

Another fun thing to do is to speak the Orphic Hymn of the planet over the talisman. I enjoy this for Jupiter talismans in particular. Just make sure you read it and think about what it means and whether your intent is actually in the hymn.

## Putting Talismans on Vacation

When you are not actively using a talisman, you can put it out to pasture by telling it thanks for all its help, and that you'll call on it again when you require its aid. This sets the thing in a dormant state and keeps your name in the spirit's list of semi-active cases. Let it rest somewhere secure and honored.

When you are ready to reactivate it, perform a consecration similar to the original consecration rite.

## Decommissioning Talismans

Sometimes, you have a talisman that you no longer want in your life. At this point, you must decommission the talisman, and return its component parts to the Earth it was made from.

The decommissioning ceremony should consist of the following:

The conjuration of the spirits over the talisman, and of the talisman itself.

An offering of thanksgiving for its help in your life, thanking it for the special moments that stand out in your mind specifically.

The farewell to the spirit, mentioning, "As these pieces of your talisman are returned to our Mother, the Spiritus Mundi, so also be free to go on your way. Remember our friendship. As you came in peace, so go in power."

When you have decommissioned the talisman, break it down to its component parts as far as you can, and scatter them to the winds, disperse them in waters, or let them be consumed in fire. You want to get it as fine as possible.

If it is a metal talisman, or something that will take longer to break down, the best thing you can do is melt it and recast it as a blank during an appropriate day and hour. If this isn't a possibility, dispose of it in running water. Note that this is not for talismans that have toxic effects, like mercury sulfate, tin, or lead. Each of these metals can be returned to a blank state on a stovetop if necessary. Silver, gold, and iron can be disposed of in running water with relatively low impact on the world around us. It's littering, but with good intent.

Anything else should be burned and scattered. Stones should be cast in shallow running water where the light of sun, moon and stars can reach it. Animal necrotic bio-matter should be buried or left out in the elements somewhere wild. Plant matter can be burned or buried. Paper seals should be burned. Clay figures should be smashed, statuary defaced. It is the act of mortality and disbursement to be formed anew in a different shape that you are enacting.

Decommissioning is not something to consider lightly. It is the death of a companion you have brought into your life. In most cases, simply putting a talisman out to pasture is the best resort. Decommissioning is only something I do when I have created a talisman with an intent that brings about an unintended and undesirable consequence.

## Planetary Talismans

The following sections go into the details necessary to create a physical talisman for each of the planets. These talismans can be placed around your Table of Practice near the names of the archangels of the spheres as a means to turn it into a manifestations device. Note that the lists of things provided for each sphere are overkill. You're creating a small bag of herbs, minerals, and other associated items. Pick the things you have available. You don't have to stuff the whole bag with herbs and such. I try to have at least a crystal point, one stone, and a couple herbs that are of the appropriate planetary nature.

## *Jupiter Talisman*

Gather the ingredients that are of a Jupiter nature. These can be found in Agrippa's chapters on the Things under Mars, or in *The Complete Magician's Tables* by Skinner. Or you could use my list that I got from these resources:

- Hyssop
- Nutmeg
- High John the Conqueror root
- Lapis Lazuli
- Amethyst
- Crystal Point
- Tobacco from your Cigar

Begin with a consecration for each of the items. You can do this by conjuring Sachiel, described in the rite discussed earlier, and when he's present lift each item in his direction and ask him to consecrate, bless, dedicate, and empower the item in the manifestation of Jupiter's powers.

When they are all consecrated, combine them together in a small cloth bag. On one side, draw the Astrological symbol of Jupiter and the Seal of Jupiter as shown in the Contemplation seals.

On the other side, draw the Seal of Johphiel, the Intelligence of the Sphere of Jupiter, and Hismael. Write their names underneath if you like. It's not necessary.

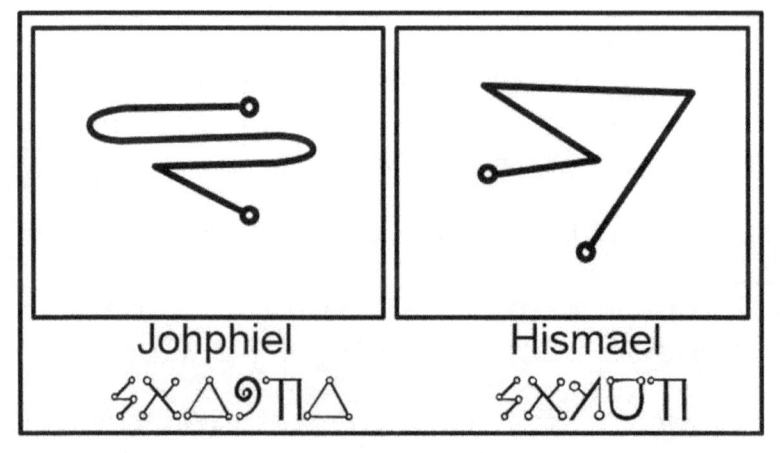

*Figure 18: Images of the Tables of the Planets Corresponding to Jupiter*

Ask Sachiel to bring you in contact with Johphiel, the Intelligence of the Table of Jupiter. When he is present, ask him to also bring Hismael, Spirit of the Table of Jupiter. (Note: if you don't sense them, don't worry, just keep going. Trust me, they're totally present.)

Ask the Intelligence to consecrate the talisman that it may radiate the forces of Jupiter directly into your sphere. Ask the Spirit to work under the guidance of the Intelligence to manifest the powers of Jupiter in your sphere, specifically mentioning, "Without bringing any harm or unnecessary stress to myself or those within my Sphere of Influence."

When you have done this, let the spirits go using the closeout portion from the rite above.

## Mars Talisman

Gather the ingredients that are of a Martial nature. These can be found in Agrippa's chapters on the Things under Mars, or in *The Complete Magician's Tables* by Skinner. Or you could use my list that I got from these resources:

- Wolf's Bane
- Laurel
- High John the Conqueror root
- Bloodstone, Jasper, Amethyst, or Garnet
- Crystal Point
- Tobacco from your Cigar

Begin with a consecration for each of the items. You can do this by conjuring Kammael, described in the rite discussed earlier, and when he's present, lift each item in his direction and ask him to consecrate, bless, dedicate, and empower the item in the manifestation of Mars' powers.

When they are all consecrated, combine them together in a small cloth bag. On one side, draw the Astrological symbol of Mars and the Seal of Mars as shown above.

On the other side, draw the Seal of Graphiel, the Intelligence of the Sphere of Mars, and Barzabel. Write their names underneath if you like. It's not necessary.

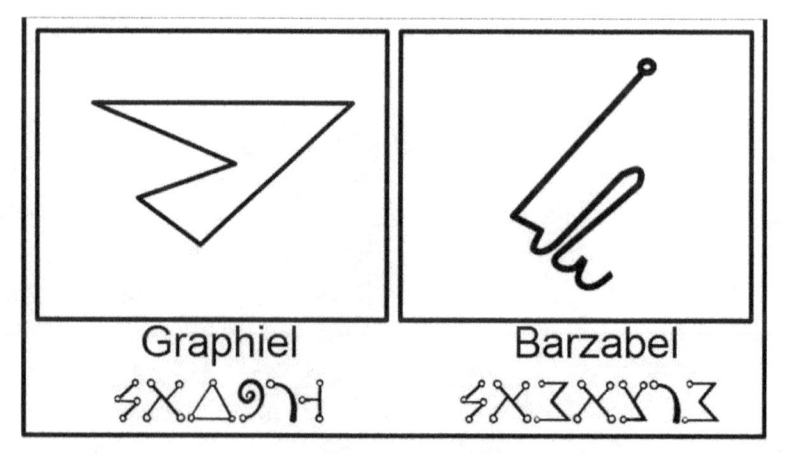

*Figure 19: Images of the Tables of the Planets Corresponding to Mars*

Ask Kammael to bring you in contact with Graphiel, the Intelligence of the Table of Mars. When he is present, ask him to also bring Barzabel, Spirit of the Table of Mars. (Note: if you don't sense them, don't worry, just keep going. Trust me, they're totally present.)

Ask the Intelligence to consecrate the talisman that it may radiate the forces of Mars directly into your sphere. Ask the Spirit to work under the guidance of the Intelligence to manifest the powers of Mars in your sphere, specifically mentioning, "Without bringing any harm or unnecessary stress to myself or those within my Sphere of Influence."

When you have done this, let the spirits go using the closeout portion from the rite above.

## Solar Talisman

When you're ready to make a Sun Talisman, here's what you need to do:

Gather the ingredients that are of The Sun's nature. These can be found in Agrippa's chapters on the things under The Sun, or in *The Complete Magician's Tables* by Skinner. Or you could select from the list that I got from these resources:

- Heliotrope, Hyacinth, Saffron, Cloves, Cinnamon, Chamomile
- Chrysolite, also known as Olivine
- Citrine, amber, or any yellow stone
- Crystal Point
- Pieces of Frankincense
- Tobacco from your Cigar

Begin with a consecration for each of the items. You can do this by conjuring Michael, described in the rite discussed earlier, and when he's present, lift each item in his direction and ask him to consecrate, bless, dedicate, and empower the item in the manifestation of the Sun's powers.

When they are all consecrated, combine them together in a small cloth bag. On one side, draw the Astrological symbol of the Sun and the Seal of the Sun as shown above.

On the other side, draw the Seal of Nachiel, the Intelligence of the Sphere of the Sun, and Sorath. Write their names underneath if you like. It's not necessary.

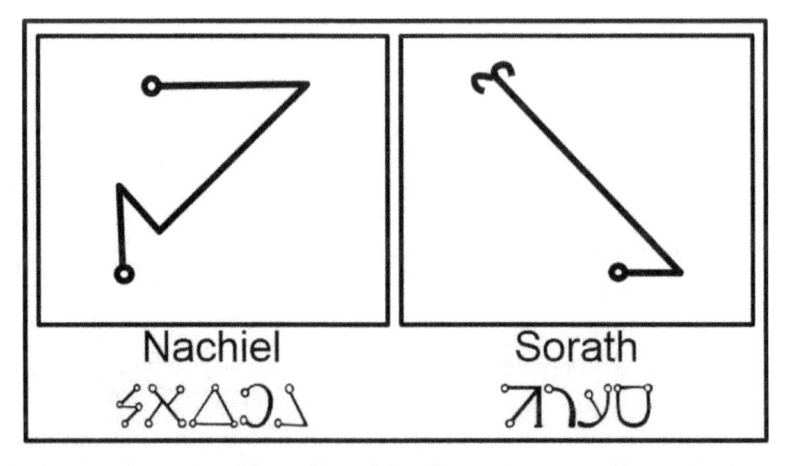

*Figure 20: Images of the Tables of the Planets Corresponding to the Sun*

Ask Michael to bring you in contact with Nachiel, the Intelligence of the Table of the Sun. When he is present, ask him to also bring Sorath, Spirit of the Table of the sun. (Note: if you don't sense them, don't worry, just keep going. Trust me, they're totally present.)

Ask the Intelligence to consecrate the talisman that it may radiate the forces of the Sun directly into your sphere. Ask the Spirit to work under the guidance of the Intelligence to manifest the powers of the Sun in your sphere, and to aid in the leadership of your Kingdom.

When you have done this, let the spirits go using the closeout portion from the rite above.

## Venus Talisman

When you're ready to make a Venus Talisman, here's what you need to do:

Gather the ingredients that are of a Venus nature. These can be found in Agrippa's chapters on the things under Venus, or in *The Complete Magician's Tables* by Skinner. Or you could select from the list that I got from these resources:

- Vervain, Violet, Valerian, Thyme, Coriander, Rose Petals, all sweet perfumes
- Beryl, Green Jasper, Carnelian, Coral
- Emerald, Sapphire
- Crystal Point
- Pieces of Sandalwood, dried pomegranate peel
- Tobacco from your Cigar

Begin with a consecration for each of the items. You can do this by conjuring Anael, described in the rite discussed earlier, and when he's present, lift each item in his direction and ask him to consecrate, bless, dedicate, and empower the item in the manifestation of Venus' powers.

When they are all consecrated, combine them together in a small cloth bag. On one side, draw the Astrological symbol of Venus and the Seal of Venus as shown above.

On the other side, draw the Seal of Hagiel, the Intelligence of the Sphere of Venus, and Kedemel, the Spirit of Venus. Write their names underneath if you like. It's not necessary.

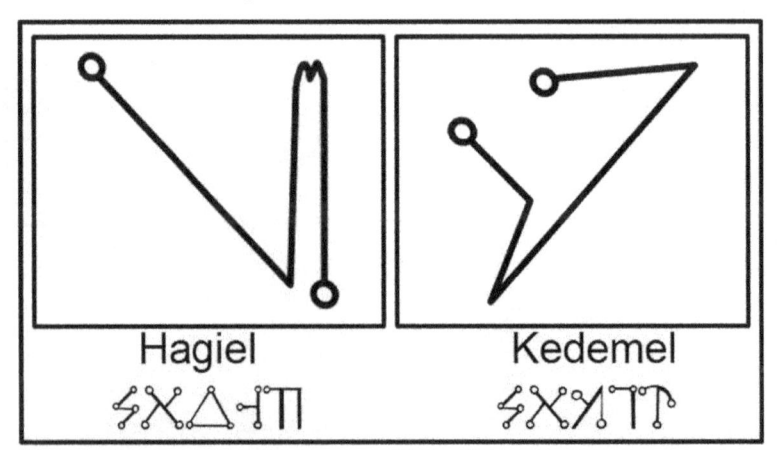

*Figure 21: Images of the Tables of the Planets Corresponding to Venus*

Ask Anael to bring you in contact with Hagiel, the Intelligence of the Table of Venus. When he is present, ask him to also bring Kedemel, Spirit of the Table of Venus. (Note: if you don't sense them, don't worry, just keep going. Trust me, they're totally present.)

Ask the Intelligence to consecrate the talisman that it may radiate the forces of Venus directly into your sphere. Ask the Spirit to work under the guidance of the Intelligence to manifest the powers of Venus in your sphere, and to aid in the leadership of your Kingdom.

When you have done this, let the spirits go using the closeout portion from the rite above.

## *Mercury Talisman*

When you're ready to make a Mercury Talisman, here's what you need to do:

Gather the ingredients that are of a Mercury nature. These can be found in Agrippa's chapters on the things under Mercury, or in *The Complete Magician's Tables* by Skinner. Or you could select from the list that I got from these resources:

- Mastic, Mace, Storax, Nutmeg, Cinquefoil (Five-Finger Grass)
- Agate, Alexandrite, Peacock Ore
- Opal
- Crystal Point
- Whole Cloves
- Tobacco from your Cigar

Begin with a consecration for each of the items. You can do this by conjuring Raphael, described in the rite discussed earlier, and when he's present, lift each item in his direction and ask him to consecrate, bless, dedicate, and empower the item in the manifestation of Mercury's powers.

When they are all consecrated, combine them together in a small cloth bag. On one side, draw the Astrological symbol of Mercury and the Seal of Mercury as shown above.

On the other side, draw the Seal of Tiriel, the Intelligence of the Sphere of Mercury, and Taphthartharath, the Spirit of Mercury. Write their names underneath if you like. It's not necessary.

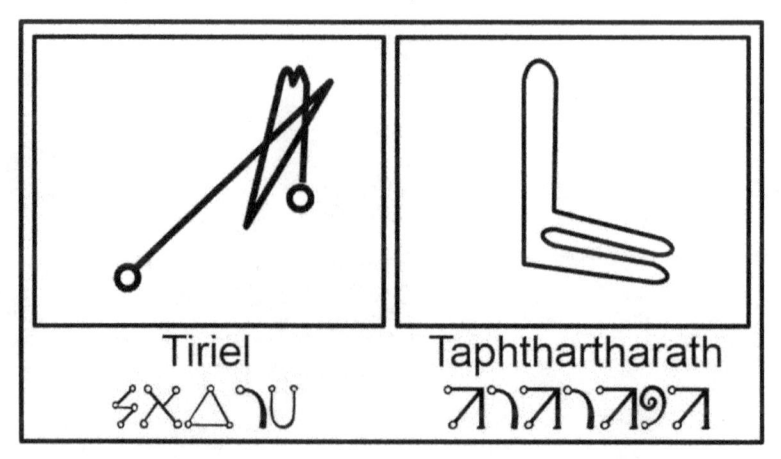

*Figure 22: Images of the Tables of the Planets Corresponding to Mercury*

Ask Mercury to bring you in contact with Tiriel, the Intelligence of the Table of Mercury. When he is present, ask him to also bring Taphthartharath, Spirit of the Table of Mercury. (Note: if you don't sense them, don't worry, just keep going. Trust me, they're totally present.)

Ask the Intelligence to consecrate the talisman that it may radiate the forces of Mercury directly into your sphere. Ask the Spirit to work under the guidance of the Intelligence to manifest the powers of Mercury in your sphere, and to aid in the leadership of your Kingdom.

When you have done this, let the spirits go using the closeout portion from the rite above.

## Lunar Talisman

When you're ready to make a Lunar Talisman, here's what you need to do:

Gather the ingredients that are of a Lunar nature. These can be found in Agrippa's chapters on the things under the Moon, or in *The Complete Magician's Tables* by Skinner. Or you could select from the list that I got from these resources:

- Crab apple, hay, camphor, cucumber, poppy, pumpkin, gourd, lettuce, melon, rampion, tamarind
- Moonstone, chalcedony
- Pearl
- Crystal Point
- Almond, Hazel, Mistletoe, lime leaves
- Tobacco from your Cigar

Begin with a consecration for each of the items. You can do this by conjuring Gabriel, described in the rite discussed earlier, and when he's present, lift each item in his direction and ask him to consecrate, bless, dedicate, and empower the item in the manifestation of the Moon's powers.

When they are all consecrated, combine them together in a small cloth bag. On one side, draw the Astrological symbol of the Moon and the Seal of the Moon as shown in the Contemplation figure in the Lunar section of the book.

On the other side, draw the Seal of Malcha betharsithim hed beruah schehakim (easy for you to say), the Intelligency of the Intelligence of the Moon, and Hasmodai, the Spirit of the Moon. Write their names underneath if you like. It's not necessary.

# Talismans

**Malcha betharsithim hed beruah schehakim**

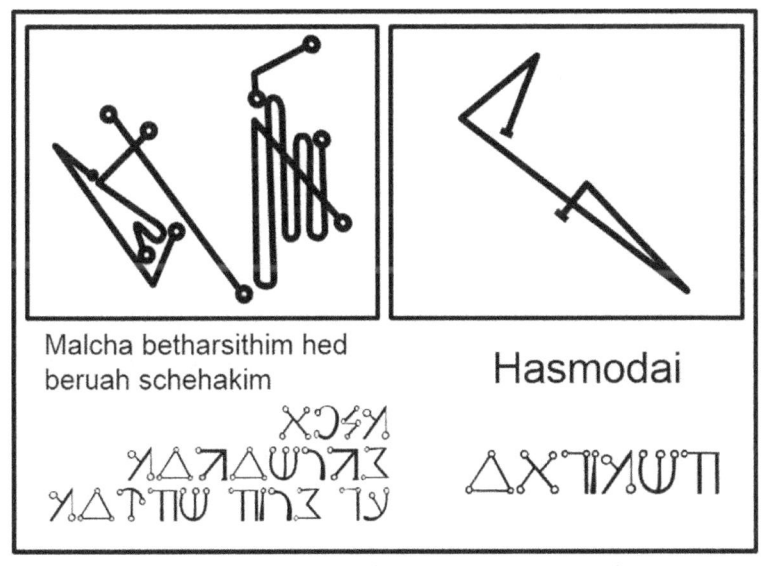

**Hasmodai**

*Figure 23: Images of the Tables of the Planets Corresponding to Luna*

Ask Gabriel to bring you in contact with Malcha betharsithim hed beruah schehakim, the Intelligency of the Intelligence of the Moon. When he is present, ask him to also bring Hasmodai, Spirit of the Table of the Moon. (Note: if you don't sense them, don't worry, just keep going. Trust me, they're totally present.)

Ask the Intelligence to consecrate the talisman that it may radiate the forces of the Moon directly into your sphere. Ask the Spirit to work under the guidance of the Intelligency to manifest the powers of the Moon in your sphere, and to aid in the leadership of your Kingdom.

When you have done this, let the spirits go using the closeout portion from the rite above.

## Saturn Talisman

When you're ready to make a Saturn Talisman, here's what you need to do:

Gather the ingredients that are of a Saturn nature. These can be found in Agrippa's chapters on the things under Saturn, or in *The Complete Magician's Tables* by Skinner. Or you could select from the list that I got from these resources:

- Daffodil, cumin, hellebore, mandrake, Opium
- Lodestone, chalcedony; also lead
- Onyx, or sapphire
- Crystal Point
- Pieces of Myrrh
- Tobacco from your Cigar

Begin with a consecration for each of the items. You can do this by conjuring Cassiel, described in the rite discussed earlier, and when he's present, lift each item in his direction and ask him to consecrate, bless, dedicate, and empower the item in the manifestation of Saturn's powers.

When they are all consecrated, combine them together in a small cloth bag. On one side, draw the Astrological symbol of Saturn and the Seal of Saturn as shown above.

On the other side, draw the Seal of Agiel, the Intelligence of the Sphere of Saturn, and Zazel. Write their names underneath if you like. It's not necessary.

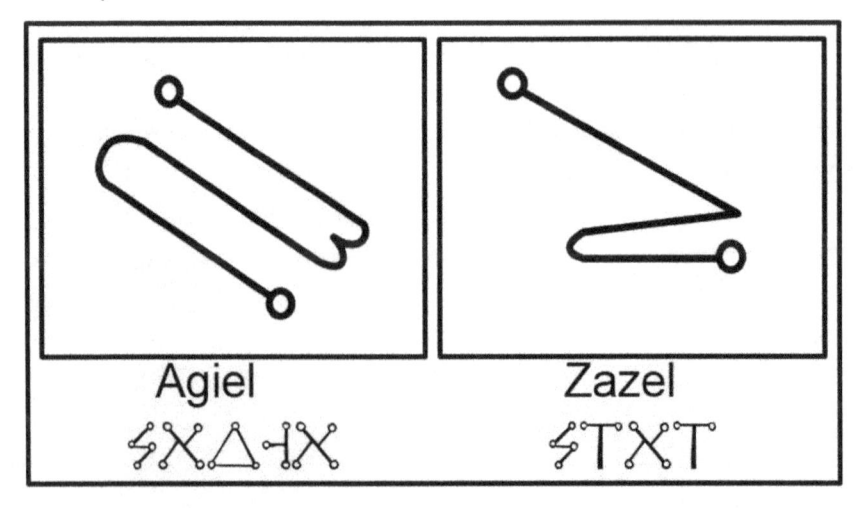

*Figure 24: Images of the Tables of the Planets Corresponding to Saturn*

Ask Cassiel to bring you in contact with Agiel, the Intelligence of the Table of Saturn. When he is present, ask him to also bring Zazel, Spirit of the Table of Saturn. (Note: if you don't sense them, don't worry, just keep going. Trust me, they're totally present.)

Ask the Intelligence to consecrate the talisman that it may radiate the forces of Saturn directly into your sphere. Ask the Spirit to work under the guidance of the Intelligence to manifest the powers of Saturn in your sphere, and to aid in the protection and expansion of the borders of your Kingdom.

When you have done this, let the spirits go using the closeout portion from the rite above.

# Afterword:
# Kingdom Maintenance and Tapping the Powers of the Spheres to Live an Awesome Life

In this book, I've talked a lot about how the forces of the spheres manifest, and the different things they rule in your Kingdom. We've gone over the basic, simple process necessary to start tapping into these forces to establish yourself as a king in your own kingdom. We've covered some pretty advanced techniques and interpretations of planetary magic that is specifically designed to set you up to understand who you are spiritually, materially, and what you're doing here from a context of eternity.

A lot of this is going to immediately manifest in your life as getting your basic fundamental aspects of your life together. You'll find yourself getting a better financial source of income. You'll find relationships that are dangerous to you falling apart to be replaced with healthy ones. You'll find yourself coming up with brilliant ideas, or seeing ways to make a difference socially on the local and global scale. You'll find that these things just sort of fall into place for a while without a lot of work required on your part beyond paying attention to opportunities, and deciding to go after what you really want.

After a while, you'll find that you've got a pretty good life, sufficient income, a nice relationship, and a good bunch of friends to work with. You'll have clout, impact, and a plan. And you'll be working towards that plan regularly. And then you'll find the inevitable obstacle, issue, problem person, or stuck area in your life.

These rites are still going to be useful to you then. You can keep using this basic structure to work with the Powers of spheres to make your world a better place.

When you've identified some aspect in your life that you specifically want to address, you take the rite and modify it, add more to it after the Orphic Hymn. In this book, we've let the Orphic Hymns be the statements of intent of the rite, because they are already phrased in the right way to heal and correct a person's sphere if it's out of balance or out of power.

But as you go through life from a position of power, you'll want to alter things to deal with what you're facing. You'll want to add instructions, ask for advice, ask for specific changes to your situation. It's not all that hard, really; you just need to be able to express what you really want to have happen in terms that make sense.

Over time you'll find yourself developing this skill naturally. You'll want something that's more expensive than your budget allows for, and you'll talk to Jupiter about a temporary increase in funds. A couple of weeks later, you'll see a chance to make the additional money you needed pop into being. Or you'll have a friend who finds they have to go into the hospital for a possible malignant tumor, and you'll be speaking to Raphael on their behalf, or Michael if it's a hidden symptom.

And as you move on in your personal Work, you'll find yourself working with other types of spirits, spirits of the terrestrial worlds, the elemental kingdoms. You may be calling on demons, or supernatural assistants. You may be wandering among the astral realms to explore and document the extra terrestrial spirits of specific constellations and their impact on the Earth below.

These rites will serve you well in those instances too. One of my favorite things about the techniques I present here is that they are fluid. If you've read my *Modern Angelic Grimoire*, you'll note the rather extreme diversion from my Trithemian based system. I've grown into the system I presented in this book, and even now the script is not something I always follow. There are ritual baths to include, with sachets of herbs floating around. There are impromptu consecrations using organic Hyssop oil. There are times I work alone, and other times I Work with a Seer.

Don't be afraid to adapt this rite to your needs. Allow your experiences to lead you to new ways of doing things.

# Afterword

Above all else, use this information to find your personal happiness, the thing that brings you joy. Look high to the highest heights, to your very Source. Set your gaze upon the One Star that you came from, in whose elements you were mingled, and to whose fires you shall return. Keep that Star in sight. Soar through the Heavens, return in power and wisdom as you see fit.

But above all else, enjoy your kingdom.

That's why you're here.